DRAGON'S GUARD

THE DRAGON SHIFTER'S MATES #1

EVA CHASE

INK SPARK PRESS

Dragon's Guard

Book 1 in the Dragon Shifter's Mates series

All rights reserved. This book or any portion thereof may not be reproduced or used in any manner without the express written permission of the author, except for the use of brief quotations in a book review.

This is a work of fiction. Any resemblance to actual persons, living or dead, or actual events is purely coincidental.

First Digital Edition, 2017

ISBN: 978-0-9959865-5-8

CHAPTER 1

Ren

"ARE YOU WAITING FOR SOMEONE, HONEY?" the bartender asked.

It was a reasonable question, considering that I'd been perched on one of the leather-cushioned seats at the bar for ten minutes without ordering anything. If the place had been any busier, he'd probably have pushed me a lot sooner. But there was only one other patron down the counter from me, a grizzled dude who was glued to his beer and the burble of the football game, and a handful of people scattered around the wooden tables in the rest of the room.

I'd picked this bar for exactly that reason. If she came, it'd be somewhere low key, not too noisy or crowded. At least, that had felt like the right idea. It wasn't as if she'd shown up anyway.

"Not exactly," I said to the bartender, leaning my

elbows on the counter. The smell of wood varnish and booze tickled my nose. "And if you're going to call me anything, call me Ren." Most of the times I'd heard "honey" in the last seven years, it'd been followed by a leer and a grope.

The bartender didn't take offense, just grinned. "No problem, Ren. Can I get you anything, while you're 'not exactly' waiting?"

I was feeling too restless to want a drink for pleasure, but maybe that was why I should have one. It'd take the edge off my nerves. "I'll have a Bloody Mary."

"That I can do." His grin turned apologetic. "I do have to ask for ID. Take it as a compliment?"

I shrugged and pulled out my wallet. When I flashed the card at him, he chuckled. "Birthday girl, huh? It's an honor to serve your first drink." He raised an eyebrow. "Or at least your first legal drink."

Yeah, we wouldn't get into the amounts of cheap vodka and rum I'd gulped for a buzz over the last several years. When you were crashing on the streets, there was always someone passing around a bottle in a paper bag. But I was done with that part of my life now.

There was only one thing still missing.

"Make it extra bloody," I told the bartender. He saluted me and grabbed a glass. As he mixed the cocktail, I looked toward the door. Beyond the window, the headlights of Brooklyn traffic streaked by through the darkening evening. No one walked in.

My hand rose to the locket that dangled just below my collarbone. I traced the delicate vine pattern etched in the warm gold. My chest still tightened a little when I flicked the locket open, even though I'd done it already a dozen times today.

The necklace was the last thing my mother had given to me. Seven years ago, but I could remember so vividly the way her dark eyes had shimmered with a hint of tears as she'd pressed the locket into my hands. She'd clasped her fingers over mine and leaned close. The perfume she wore, like smoky roses, had filled my lungs.

"I have to go," she'd said. "If what I'm about to do works out the way I hope, I'll be back before you know it. But if I'm not... You hold onto this locket. Don't take it off for an instant. And keep it closed until your twenty-first birthday. Then, if I'm not here, you open it."

At the time, turning twenty-one had felt so distant I'd hardly processed what she was saying. She'd left before on her little trips, but she'd never been gone more than a week or two. When she'd pulled me into her arms, I'd hugged her back a little harder than usual, but I hadn't really believed she wouldn't come back. She was the one sure thing I'd always had.

But she hadn't come back. And here I was, twenty-one. I snapped the locket closed, nudged it open, snapped it closed again. There was nothing inside but another etching, this one a symbol like an upside-down flame at the heart of a spiraling line. It didn't mean anything to me. I wasn't sure if it was supposed to.

Somewhere in the back of my head, I'd had the idea that the second I'd open the locket, Mom would know. She'd know, and she'd come find me. Whatever had been stopping her before, it'd be over.

I'd braced myself and popped it open for the first

time twelve hours ago. And here I was, still twenty-one, sitting alone in a half-empty bar on a Thursday night.

Not alone for long. The bartender set my Bloody Mary down in front of me, and a guy who'd been sitting at one of the tables ambled over. He plopped onto the stool next to mine, called to the bartender for a gin and tonic, and looked me up and down.

"You seem to be a little lonely tonight, sweetheart," he said. His voice sounded as greasy as his hair looked. The armpits of his dress shirt were ringed with sweat stains. "Maybe I can help with that."

Hard pass on that one. "I'm good, actually," I said. "No assistance required."

He shuffled a little closer. He smelled like sweat too—sweat and the three to four drinks he'd already downed. Ugh. "Aw, come on. No harm in a little conversation."

I wouldn't be so sure about that, I thought. The truth was, even if he'd been remotely appealing, I'd have steered clear. Me and guys didn't seem to mix well. I'd had a few hook-ups over the years, but nothing that had gone past second base. As soon as things took a hot and heavy turn, a strange sensation rose up inside me. Like claws digging into my innards. And I'd suddenly feel as if I could rip the guy apart.

As if maybe I wanted to.

There's nothing like visions of gruesome murder to put a damper on your libido.

That wasn't the only time I felt the stirring of those claws inside me. The greasy guy tapped me on the shoulder with a smirk, and a prickle crept up over my ribs. The picture he was presenting snapped together into sudden focus. I could almost taste his bruised ego in its sauce of desperation.

"I'm not any more interested than your ex is," I said, and took a sip of my Bloody Mary. "So how about you leave both of us alone?"

The guy's face turned sallow. "Bitch," he muttered. He snatched his drink off the counter and stalked away.

I swallowed another mouthful of the spicy, tomatoey cocktail. The bartender had made sure it packed a good wallop, exactly the way I wanted. Enough to wash away most of the discomfort of that encounter.

My phone vibrated in my pocket. I pulled it out and smiled when I saw the name on the screen. "Hey, Kylie!" I said. "Are you really supposed to be making calls in the middle of your shift?"

"I made a deal with my supervisor that I'd cut out early tonight in exchange for an extra long shift tomorrow," my best friend said in her chirpy voice. "Birthday surprise! Where are you, Ren? We need to rock tonight, hard."

I laughed. Maybe this was what I really needed. Mom was long gone, doing whatever had been more important than sticking with her only kid, and of course no piece of jewelry was going to bring her back. But I didn't need her anymore. I'd gotten through the last seven years alive if not completely unscathed, and now Kylie and I had finally scrounged together enough money to put a down payment on an apartment.

It was a crappy apartment, on a street so seedy there were more weeds than concrete on the sidewalks, but it had four walls and a ceiling with no holes. It had a door with a lock, and only we had the keys. These days, that was heaven.

Kylie normally worked the evening and early night shift cashiering and stocking shelves at a rundown grocery store in the 'hood. I'd be back hauling boxes at my warehouse job tomorrow morning. No fun, but whatever paid the bills. And I could sleepwalk through the job, so I didn't need to worry about a hangover.

I turned around one of the coasters sitting on the counter to check the bar's name. "I'm at a place called Carmello's," I said. "It's on 5th Ave a few blocks from the park. But I can meet you wherever."

"No, no," Kylie said. "I'm coming to get you. And then I'm taking you on one epic adventure, little girl."

"I'll hold you to that promise," I said. Not that I had any doubt Kylie would deliver. She was only a couple years older than me, but when I'd first run into her a few years back, that had seemed like a much bigger gap than it did now. She'd looked out for me as much a big sister as a friend.

Carmello's would definitely be too much of a snore for her to want to stick around here. I gulped some more of my Bloody Mary so I'd be finished before she showed up.

The door sighed open, too early for it to be Kylie already. My heart leapt despite the talking-to I'd given myself. But it definitely wasn't my mom walking in.

The guy looked young, maybe mid-twenties, but there was a confidence in the way he prowled into the bar that seemed to carry the weight of a lot more experience. His round face was broken by the jut of sharp cheekbones—not exactly handsome, but definitely memorable. His hazel eyes swept the room and came to rest on me.

I jerked my gaze away, realizing I'd been staring. And he wasn't at all the kind of person I wanted to be staring at. Living on the streets had given me a keen instinct for danger. This guy? He was not someone to mess with. A sense of purpose radiated off of him too. I figured it was better not to get in the way of whatever he was up to.

Just my luck, he sauntered up to the bar right beside me. "Give me the best thing you have on tap," he said to the bartender, and turned toward me. "Nice night to be out on the town."

"I suppose," I said noncommittally. How long was it going to take Kylie to get here and give me an easy exit?

Cheekbones cocked his head. "All the early summer energy in the air, it really brings the beast out."

What was *that* supposed to mean? I shrugged and acted fascinated by my Bloody Mary. He didn't take the hint.

"Maybe we could take a walk, get to know each other a little better."

I cut my eyes toward him. He *was* confident, wasn't he? My quick tongue got a little ahead of my better judgment. "Who says I'm looking to get to know you?"

Cheekbones grinned at me, looking unfazed. "I'm just saying, we clearly have a lot in common. This isn't our kind of place, is it? Why not come back to the fold, at least for a visit?"

A lot in common? The fold? Was this guy *on* something? No dilated pupils, no jerky movements, but you never knew what drugs were making the rounds these days.

I drained as much of my drink as I could in one swallow and set down the glass. The hit of spice and alcohol sharpened my inner claws. "I'm pretty sure we have exactly nothing in common," I said. "For one thing, I know how to take a 'No.'"

Before I had to find out how he was going to answer that, I hopped off my stool and made a beeline for the back hall with its *Restrooms* sign. He wasn't likely to follow me into the ladies'.

Washing my hands, I peered at my reflection. I hadn't put on anything other than my standard mascara and light maroon lipstick combo today. I was dressed casual in a faded Nine Inch Nails tee and jeans. I'd been blessed with a good hair day, my chocolate-brown waves drifting artfully across my shoulders the way I usually struggled and failed to style them, but otherwise nothing extra special was going on. So why were guys honing in on me like flies to a jar of sugar water?

It didn't matter. Cheekbones made me too uneasy. Either he was drugged out or partly insane, and neither would lead to a good outcome. I'd text Kylie to meet me at the all-ages club on the other side of town and grab a cab to be on my way.

I was reaching for my phone as I came out of the restroom, and a pair of arms slammed around me from behind. One clapped a damp cloth over my face. The other wrapped around my waist. A sickly sweet smell washed over me. I swung back my elbow—and the world went black.

CHAPTER 2

Ren

I woke up with a muddy feeling behind my eyes and velvety fabric against my cheek. Neither of those sensations felt right.

Blinking, I rubbed my forehead. The room around me came into focus. It still didn't make much sense.

I was lying on a four-poster bed in an elegantly decorated bedroom. Thin sunlight drifted in past the brocade curtains on either side of a wide window. The bedframe, as well as the dresser and the vanity by the walls, looked like mahogany, polished to a shine. Gold flower patterns glinted on the mint-green wallpaper.

The bedspread under me was actually velvet. The soft pile darkened under the pressure of my hands as I pushed myself upright. A sweet lilac scent drifted up from it.

Sweet. The memory rushed up of the arms catching

me, the cloth over my nose and mouth. My pulse stuttered. I touched my face as if I could pull that moment out of my past. Make it not have happened.

But it had happened. Someone had grabbed me and knocked me out. And brought me here, wherever *here* was. Apparently my kidnapper had a lot of money and a decadent taste in furnishings.

I patted my pockets. My phone was gone. At least my clothes were all still on and in order. I didn't feel any unexpected aches or pains. No reason to think I'd been manhandled other than that initial assault.

At least so far. Who knew what my kidnapper had planned for me next?

Muscles tensed, I pushed myself off the bed. The window appeared to be at the front of the house. It looked out over a suburban street. A wide lawn led down to the road, and a large Victorian home stood on the far side, maybe a hundred feet away. There was another house in view to the left, beyond a thick hedge. I didn't see anyone moving in their windows or outside, but the sun had just risen over the horizon. I might get a chance to yell for help later.

In the meantime, I treaded across the floorboards to the vanity, looking for a letter opener or hairpin or anything else reasonably stabby. The drawers revealed only pots and tubes of various makeup powders and creams, a brush and a comb, and a mirror in a silver case that was smaller than my palm.

Footsteps sounded outside the door. My hand stuffed the mirror in my pocket automatically. Spend a few years thieving and it becomes an impulse. I shoved the drawer closed and backed toward the window.

The doorknob turned. There was no click of a key or scrape of a deadbolt. I hesitated despite my thudding heart. The door hadn't even been locked? I hadn't bothered to check, I'd been so sure it would be.

The door glided open. A guy I'd never seen before strolled into the room. I was sure of that, because if I *had* seen him before, even years ago, I definitely would have remembered him. He was the most gorgeous human being I'd ever set eyes on.

A sleekly muscular body, at least a few inches taller than my five-foot-nine, filled out his fitted dress shirt and slacks. His face was sleek too, with deep indigo-blue eyes and a topping of spiky black hair. The only feature that marred its perfect symmetry was a small scar that nicked his left eyebrow, but somehow that only made him look more perfect. An earring gleamed in his right earlobe—a tiny sapphire stud that matched his eyes.

He stopped a couple steps into the room and offered me a crooked grin. A flutter raced through my chest.

Holy hell. I'd been knocked out and carted off into some stranger's house. This was not the time for melting panties, Ren.

And yet they were melting. My heart was still thumping, but it wasn't entirely fear now. The quiver running through my nerves felt more like eager anticipation.

What the hell was wrong with me?

And was it my imagination, or was the guy staring back at me just as avidly?

"Welcome to my home," he said in a jaunty, melodic voice. "I'm sorry we had to meet under these circumstances. I promise you, kidnapping isn't my usual style. I was hoping to speak with you in your own territory. My assistant got a little... overenthusiastic."

He cut a glance toward the doorway. I *had* seen the guy standing there before. It was Cheekbones, from the bar. My shoulders stiffened.

But after all his swaggering in the bar, he now looked totally deflated. He shuffled over the room's threshold and dropped to his knees, bowing his head.

"I am so sorry. I overstepped."

"By a *huge* margin," the first guy said dryly.

"By a huge margin," Cheekbones leapt to agree. "It was completely my fault. I wasn't even supposed to talk to you. I— Again, I'm sorry."

"All right," his boss said with a flick of his hand. "Get going. I'm sure she doesn't want to see your face any more than she has to. You can get started with your new job." He turned back to me with that slanted smile. "I've assigned him to cleaning duty for a month, which seemed to make sense, considering what a mess he made of things."

"I'm confused," I said. "I— So you didn't *mean* to kidnap me?" It was a little hard to wrap my head around that idea.

"Like I said, not my style. I'd have told Leonard to bring you back to your home if I'd known where that was. Since I didn't"—he motioned to the room—"I tried to make you as comfortable as possible in the meantime."

He hadn't come any closer, still giving me plenty of

space. But he was standing between me and the doorway. I wet my lips.

"So, if I wanted to, I could go home right now?"

The guy's eyebrows lifted. "Well, of course. Be my guest to stop being my guest." He sidestepped to open the way to the door. "We're only a half hour from Brooklyn, and there's a train station a ten minute walk down the street. But maybe you'll consider accepting my hospitality for a little longer, now that you're here and all? I've been waiting a very long time to get the chance to talk to you."

I'd already crossed half the room. At that comment, my body froze up. I stared at him. "What do you mean? You said that before: that you wanted to talk to me. Talk to me about *what*? Who *are* you? Why were you—and your 'assistant'—poking around in my life at all?"

"Let's take those one at a time, starting with the simplest. My name is Marco. Pleased to meet you." He dipped his head in a playful half bow. "I'd like to talk to you about pretty much everything, but maybe starting with what you've been doing for the last sixteen years. And do you really have no idea why I'd be interested?"

Marco said the last bit lightly, but his indigo gaze held mine intently. That shiver of anticipation ran through my nerves again. Randomly I found myself wondering what one of those agile hands would feel like tracing over my skin—

Okay, Ren, mind out of the gutter. You've known this guy exactly five minutes, and you can't even be sure this whole kidnapping thing was really accidental.

Other than the fact that I *believed* him, right down in

the core of me, for reasons I couldn't explain. *He wouldn't lie to me*, my gut said. How the hell could I know that?

None of those reactions answered his question, though. "No," I said. "I haven't got a clue. This isn't some kind of birthday prank that Kylie set up, is it?" It seemed awfully elaborate—and freaky—even for her.

Marco shook his head. "No. Definitely not a prank. I'm just trying to make things right."

"With *me*? But I've never met you before. I've never even seen you before."

"Haven't we met? Your name is Serenity, isn't it?"

I hadn't thought I could tense up any more than I already was. It turned out I was wrong. My back went completely rigid.

No one used that name. No one had used it except my mother, in the quietest whispers when I was sick or drifting off to sleep, in as long as I could remember.

"My name is Ren," I said. My voice came out in a rasp.

"Short for Serenity," Marco said. "You don't need to hide it with me. I'm not going to hurt you."

Why would he say that? My thoughts were spinning. I pressed my hand to my forehead. Marco stepped toward me.

"I don't understand any of this," I said. "I really don't."

His expression softened. As I dropped my hand, he raised his to touch my cheek. My pulse hiccupped, but with the urge to lean into his touch, not to pull away. My skin tingled beneath his fingers. A rich, spicy smell like cinnamon-spiked coffee wafted off of him. Delicious. My gaze dropped to his mouth.

His Adam's apple bobbed. "What did she do to you, my Princess of Flames?" he murmured. "How has she shut you away?"

"No one shut me away," I said. "I'm right here. Who are you talking about?"

"Your mother. It had to be her. To protect you, of course, but—"

I jerked back, my eyes widening. "What do you know about my mother? *How* do you know anything about her?"

Marco looked just as startled by my outburst as I felt. "You could say we ran in the same circles a long time ago. I've been looking for her just as much as you."

The hope that had started to bubble up inside me burst. "Then you don't know where she is now."

He frowned. "No. Don't you? Ren, I think you'd better—" He drew in a sharp breath and summoned his earlier jaunty tone. "I'm being a horrible host. All this talk over breakfast time and not offering you a single thing to eat. I'll bring something up for you. Why don't you take a moment to clear your head? It seems we have more to talk about than I realized."

He lifted my hand to give it a peck on the back. The brush of his lips left my skin burning. Then he swept out of the room without waiting for my response.

CHAPTER 3

Marco

Leonard, the idiot, was hanging around in the hall. "What are you doing?" I snarled as I strode past him. "I told you to get started on your cleaning detail."

He hurried after me, looking bewildered. "I thought you were joking about that, Marco."

"Oh, really?" I spun on him at the top of the staircase. "Did you also think I was joking when I reamed you out for going up to my friend in there and trying to investigate on your own? Not to mention dragging her out here against her will? Or did that part, at least, sink in?"

Leonard cringed. With anyone else, he would have blustered back, but I knew he was a coward at heart. He crumbled in the face of a stronger authority.

Unfortunately I hadn't been around to exert that authority last night. *Track the source of the magic as closely as possible,* I'd told him. *I'll take over from there when I make it up from North Carolina.* Apparently those instructions hadn't been clear enough. My New York lieutenant had gotten it into his head that I'd be impressed if he brought the girl in on his own. Because kidnapping was obviously the perfect way to rebuild the trust that had been so brutally lost.

But she didn't seem to remember there was anything to rebuild. She'd responded to me—I'd caught her reaction, that immediate draw toward one's mate. The same thing I'd felt the second I'd laid eyes on her. And, God, what a beauty of a mate I had. The smell of her, sweet and tart at the same time, when I'd leaned close to her... It'd taken all my self-control not to lower my lips to hers, to find out if she tasted just as good.

She wasn't ready for that. She wasn't ready for any of this. Her *body* had responded, but her confusion had been genuine. She didn't even recognize what I was, and I was pretty sure she didn't know what *she* was either. My Princess of Flames, without a clue she was anything other than an ordinary human being. You couldn't get much more absurd than that.

And now I had to try to explain it to her on top of justifying my lieutenant's unfortunate kidnapping tendencies.

I glowered at Leonard a little more, but really, the fault was at least half mine for picking him for the job.

"The other alphas will be on their way," I said. "They could arrive any minute. So now that you know I'm not joking, please find a lamp to dust or a toilet to scrub."

"Yes, sir. I'm sorry, sir." Leonard bobbed his head and

loped away. Maybe he could learn. I didn't enjoy hearing my underlings simper, but it was better than them running around half-cocked—and fucking up the most important moment in my life so far.

I headed downstairs, picking up the scent of frying sausages and scrambled eggs from the kitchen. Lindy, who took care of this house during the long periods when I was situated elsewhere, had known we were going to need breakfast even if I'd forgotten. She was sharp enough that she'd probably already made enough for guests.

Under the sounds of sizzling oil and a spatula tapping the pans, a creaking reached my feline-sharp ears. I stopped, turning my head to zero in on the noise.

The back parlor. Someone was trying to jimmy open the window from outside.

First kidnapping and then breaking and entering. This really was shaping up to be a fantastic day. I sucked in a breath.

"Leonard!" I shouted, making for the front hall. "I've got another job for you after all."

Ren

What did she do to you, my Princess of Flames? How has she shut you away?

Marco's words echoed in my head. I leaned it into my hands where I was sitting on the edge of the bed. My mind hadn't stopped reeling since he'd walked out the door. Which he'd left open, so I guessed I *was* allowed to leave if I wanted to. I just didn't see how I could when there were so many questions *I* needed answered now.

How had he known my mother? Why did he think he knew me? How had he found out my full name? What was so important that he'd tracked me down—that his "assistant" had thought it was worth kidnapping me over?

Why did I feel the urge to walk into his arms every second I was near him?

A yelp from outside broke through my whirling thoughts. There was a thump and a grunt, sounds of a struggle. I was already on my feet hurrying to the window when a familiar chirpy voice, hardened with anger, carried through the glass.

"Let me go! And you'd better let Ren go too. I know you took her in there. You freaking assholes. I called the police! They'll be here any time now."

Kylie. What was she doing here? I dashed the rest of the way to the window.

Kylie's neon pink pixie cut flashed in the brightening sunlight. Marco's assistant Leonard had tackled her to the ground with her arms pinned behind her back. She squirmed against him, still yelling threats and insults even though her face was pressed against the grass. Marco stood over the two of them. His mouth moved, but I couldn't make out what he was saying to Leonard.

A chill washed over me. Marco had claimed the kidnapping was accidental, but he did at least hire guys who thought that kind of behavior was a-okay. What if he hurt Kylie—or worse?

I yanked up the window and kicked out the screen.

Then, in a blink, I'd leapt onto the ledge and vaulted myself out into the air.

The wind rushed past me with the exhilaration a good jump always brought. Like a surge of power I could almost grasp hold of before it slipped through my fingers. My body hunched over, braced for impact. I hit the ground with a *thunk* that rattled my bones but didn't break any. I'd done worse.

When I scrambled to my feet, Marco was staring at me with those intoxicating indigo eyes. He glanced from me to the window and back again. Then he laughed. "If you wanted to come down, I do have a perfectly good staircase."

I ignored the quip. Leonard had frozen to watch what was going on, but he still had Kylie jammed against the lawn. "Don't hurt her," I said. "Let her go. She's my best friend."

Marco arched an eyebrow at me. "I caught your best friend attempting to break into my home."

"Because I caught *you* dragging Ren off to do who knows what to her," Kylie snapped back. She managed to tip her head at an angle so she could meet my eyes. "Are you okay?"

"I'm fine," I said. Physically speaking, at least. Emotionally... My confusion had faded behind that sharp scrabbling feeling in my chest, which was getting stronger every second Kylie lay pinned on the ground. Leonard was only following orders. I glared at Marco. "I said, *Let her go.* She was only trying to help me. You can't blame her for that."

Something shifted in his eyes as he gazed back at me.

A deeper heat than before collected between my legs. It *really* wasn't fair that this dude could make my panties melt with just one look, even when I was totally pissed off at him.

At least he listened. He raised his hand. "Leonard, that's enough."

He spoke smoothly and evenly, but his assistant jerked back as if Marco had barked the order. Kylie shoved herself upright, swiping at the bits of grass clinging to her tank top and bleached cutoffs. The second she was on her feet, she grabbed me in a hug. I squeezed her back, feeling steady for the first time since I'd woken up.

The sensation didn't last. Marco cleared his throat. "Can I ask your friend exactly how she found us?"

Kylie drew back, but she kept one arm slung around me protectively. She was half a foot shorter than me and wiry besides that, but I knew how fiercely she could fight if she had to.

"I was coming to the bar to meet up with Ren," she said. "And I saw your guy here stuffing her in the back of a car. She was obviously unconscious. He drove off before I caught up, but I got the license plate. From there..." Her lips curled into a smirk. "Let's just say I know people who know how to get into the right databases. And traffic cams are awesome."

Marco's gaze flicked to the traffic lights at the end of the long suburban block. He shook his head, looking almost amused. Kylie really did know people—lots of people. Pretty much anything you needed, she could find someone who could do it. She'd racked up a lot of favors over the years.

Believe me, I don't even like most of 'em, she'd said to me one time, halfway through a bottle of cheap wine. *But it's better getting in with people and knowing how far you can trust 'em than never knowing what they might be up to.*

"And are the police actually on their way?" Marco asked.

"Wouldn't you like to know," Kylie shot back, but I could tell from the twitch of her eyes that she was bluffing. Neither of us had a whole lot of faith in cops. She'd been trying to rescue me on her own.

It seemed Marco could read the lie too. "Well, you've found Ren, and you can see that she's all right," he said. "The situation is complicated. And it doesn't involve you. So as wonderful as it was that you dropped by, I'll have to ask you to leave now."

Kylie jutted out her chin. "Uh-uh. No way. There's obviously something sketchy going on here. Come on, Ren. Let's vamoose."

We could. Marco didn't make any move to stop me, just looked at me questioningly. Waiting to see what I would do. Seeing that strengthened my resolve.

"I can't go yet," I told Kylie. "I need to talk with Marco some more."

She tugged me around to face her. "Are you kidding me? The guy seems like a total scammer."

I swallowed hard. "He knows something about my mom," I said.

Kylie's eyes widened. I didn't talk about Mom very

much with anyone, but my best friend had heard by far the most. And she was good at reading me even when I didn't want to show how I was feeling, so she probably had a better idea of how much my mother's disappearance haunted me than I'd have liked.

"Okay," she said. "I get that. But I don't want to leave you alone with these dudes either. If you're staying, I'm staying."

Of course she'd say that. My throat tightened. There wasn't any point in arguing with her. I turned to Marco. "Anything you're going to say to me, Kylie can hear it too. That's the deal."

We stared each other down for half a minute. Then Marco chuckled. "All right. This should be interesting. Come on in. We'll have a brunch party."

He sauntered back to the front door without even checking to see if we were going to follow. I made a face at his back, but I hurried along behind him. Kylie wrapped her hand around mine.

"You're sure he's legit?" she murmured to me.

"He knew things he couldn't otherwise." Like my full name, which I'd never told even Kylie. And that it'd been sixteen years since Mom and I had come to the city.

A memory swam up from my birthday just a couple days after we'd first arrived in our East Village apartment, the rooms still bare, a cake with five candles on the floor between Mom and me. *Make a wish. You can ask for anything you want. We're starting new.*

Marco led us into a sitting room on the first floor. Like the bedroom I'd woken up in, the furniture was all tasteful, expensive-looking antiques. Kylie and I sat next to each other on a velvet-cushioned settee.

A middle-aged woman with tightly curled gray-blond hair glided into the room and set plates heaped with sausages, scrambled eggs, and buttered toast on the mahogany coffee table in front of us. The hearty smell set my mouth watering. I hadn't eaten since yesterday's mid-afternoon snack. I grabbed one of the plates and a fork that looked like actual *silver*ware and dug in.

Kylie eyed the spread. "Shit, that does look good." She picked up a plate and shoveled a forkful of eggs into her mouth. Her eyes rolled back with an ecstatic expression. Then she jabbed her fork toward Marco. He was leaning against the mantle of the empty fireplace, his arms casually crossed in front of him, watching us with a little smile.

"So what's your news about Ren's mom?" Kylie said. "We've got ears even if we're eating."

I lifted my head, gulping a piece of sausage. Marco ran his thumb over his perfect, firm lips. I was definitely not thinking about what it'd be like to kiss them while I waited on the edge of my seat for his answer. My heart had started thudding again.

"Maybe first I should ask what *you* know about her," he said in his usual light tone.

"Not much," Kylie said. "Only what Ren's told me. She was already out of the picture when I came into it."

"I'm getting the impression she's been 'out of the picture' for a while." Marco glanced at me for confirmation.

I nodded, hesitant to offer any details. I still didn't

know enough about this guy to be sure how far I could trust him. "She took a lot of trips out of the city," I said. "The last time, she didn't come home."

"And how long ago was that?"

"Do you really need me to tell you that, or do you already know?"

The serious expression I'd only glimpsed once before came back, a brief shadow across his handsome face. "I promise you, I'm not playing a game here. I want to understand what's happened as much as you do. I'm hoping that between the two of us we can put together enough pieces to see the entire picture."

He sounded sincere. I didn't sense any emotions in his stance other than concern and a little frustration, which I guessed was understandable. But he'd still told *me* barely anything.

"Why don't you—" I started.

Marco's head twitched to the side as if he'd heard a sound. A second later, it reached my ears too: the faint rumble of a car engine. He strode to the door.

"I'm sorry," he said. "Your friend is only the first of the guests coming to see you today. You're a popular girl."

He winked at me and slipped out into the hall.

CHAPTER 4

Ren

"You know this situation is totally wacko, right?" Kylie said, leaning back in the settee. She popped a folded piece of toast into her mouth and chewed vigorously. I'd never figured out how she could eat to rival a linebacker and keep that wiry frame.

"Yeah, that had occurred to me a few hundred times." I rubbed my forehead. "I'm so sorry I got you mixed up in it, Ky."

She gave me a gentle kick to the knee. "Don't be ridiculous. I'm glad I'm here. I can help you get out if things turn even more wacko. And I am kind of curious to find out the big mystery about your mom too."

"If Marco actually does know anything about her." It was starting to sound as if he hadn't seen her in even longer than I had. But the way he'd talked to me—the way he'd *looked* at me... There was something he knew, something big, that he hadn't told me yet.

Was that why my body was responding to his presence so enthusiastically? I'd never had such an intense reaction to a guy before. Of course, I couldn't say I'd ever met a guy half that gorgeous before...

As if reading my mind, Kylie arched her eyebrows. "I've got to say, you have amazing luck in mysterious sort-of kidnappers. That guy is smokin'."

I had to laugh, even as my cheeks flushed. "Yeah, I noticed that too."

"Ooh." Kylie gave me another nudge with her foot. "Maybe Ren has ulterior motives for sticking around. I'm shocked. You never go gaga over guys."

"I've never seen a guy like that," I muttered.

On the other side of the house, the front door thumped shut. I strained my ears to make out Marco's voice or our new arrival's, but I couldn't hear either. What had he meant when he'd said people were coming to see *me*? How did these other "guests" fit in with whatever secret he hadn't spilled yet?

The uncertainty overwhelmed my hunger. I'd cleared half the plate anyway. I set it down on the coffee table. The growl of another car engine carried through the walls, stopping outside. I shifted on the seat. What were they talking about out there?

My hand rose to my locket. It'd been my touchstone for comfort over the last seven years. All those years of waiting until I was allowed to open it.

I'd opened it... and before the end of the day, Marco's assistant had shown up. I peered at the etched gold oval.

That connection hadn't occurred to me before. But how could my opening the locket have brought Marco, or anyone else, my way?

I clicked it open and looked at the symbol inside. *What were you trying to tell me, Mom? Why did you make me wait to see this? I don't understand anything.*

"You opened it!" Kylie said, sitting up. Right. I hadn't seen her since I first had. She leaned over, and I held it up for her to inspect.

"I don't suppose that picture means anything to you," I said.

"Nope. Should it?"

"I don't know." Just one question on my rapidly growing list.

The necklace wasn't giving me any reassurance now. I reached to my pocket instead, feeling the hard circle of the mirror I'd pocketed upstairs. I pulled it out and ran my thumb over the cool, polished surface. My nerves settled a little.

I didn't like to think about all the minor thefts I'd carried out when I was younger, but being able to just *take* what I wanted, when I wanted, still gave me a sense of control. And I needed that sense badly right now.

A third car pulled up outside. My shoulders tensed. How many people were coming? When was Marco going to bring me into this gathering that was apparently all about me?

"You don't think this is some kind of organized crime thing, do you?" Kylie asked. "Did your mom ever seem like she was into anything shady?"

My stomach twisted at the thought. "I guess she

could have been," I said. "We were almost always together, but she did take those trips, and she could have arranged jobs over the phone." She had always seemed tense, and a little sad, when she got back from the trips. More so with every one. "She was always super-careful about us keeping a low profile. Not doing anything that might attract attention. But she acted like she was more worried about *me* than herself."

And from what I could remember, she hadn't given off that jaded vibe I'd gotten from every criminal I'd ever met. The one I probably gave off at least a little now, even though I'd left that part of my life behind.

Voices filtered through the sitting room door. I stuffed the mirror back into my pocket. The hairs on the back of my neck stood up, but at the same time the thrum of anticipation I'd felt when I'd first seen Marco raced through me, even stronger than before.

It was time. It was finally time. For what, I couldn't have said. But that was what my body believed.

Marco opened the door. He dipped his head with a smile that looked apologetically self-deprecating. "The gang's all here." Then he stepped inside, leaving the door open for his guests to follow him in.

Just a few minutes ago I'd been commenting to Kylie that I'd never seen a guy as hot as Marco before. Now, suddenly, I was faced with *four* stunningly gorgeous men.

Marco ambled across the room and stopped behind an armchair, resting his muscular forearms on its arched back. The guy who came in after him was even more buff, with broad, well-built shoulders and a brawny chest that filled out his towering frame. His dark brown eyes were even more intense than the rich chestnut of his hair.

Mr. Buff's gaze shot straight to me, and a warm smile curled his lips. An electric tingle raced over my skin. He crossed the room in a few deliberate, powerful strides and stopped a few feet from Marco, his eyes still trained on me.

The next guy walked in at a faster clip. He was stockier, but with equally broad shoulders and a devastatingly strong jaw. The regal grace of his strides made him seem just as tall as the others. The sunlight streaming through the window made his pale hair gleam gold as a Disney prince's. He stopped in the middle of the room, fixing me with a crystal-clear blue gaze that felt hopeful and searching at the same time.

The last guy stalked in with a wary air that drew my eyes to him. What did *he* have to be worried about? He halted just inside and propped himself against the doorframe, crossing his arms over his leanly muscled chest. Even though he didn't look any older than the others, mid-to-late twenties at most, strands of silver streaked his light auburn hair, which fell to just below his earlobes. They gave a slightly mystical quality to his otherwise gritty good looks. When he finally looked at me, his forest-green eyes were so penetrating I felt pinned in place.

My heart beat even faster. They were here. I didn't know why that mattered, but every nerve in my body was jittering with exhilaration. I could hardly catch my breath.

Kylie shot me a glance that said, *Can you believe these guys?*

No. No, I couldn't. But here they were.

And they were *mine*.

Where had *that* bizarre thought come from? I frowned, but before I could sort out the whirlwind of thoughts and emotions rushing through me, Marco straightened up. He gave me a knowing look, as if he could tell exactly what was going through my head.

"Here we are," he said in his languid drawl. "Happy, Dopey, Doc, and Grumpy, at your service."

The wary guy by the door—who looked like he fit the title "Grumpy" just fine—turned his head to glare at Marco. Our host grinned back. "Excuse me. You already know my name, Ren. Let me introduce you to Nate, Aaron, and West."

"'Ren'?" Grumpy-West repeated in an incredulous tone. Even so, my name in his low, throaty voice sent a shiver of pleasure down my spine.

"As she would prefer to be called," Marco said.

Dopey-Nate nodded. "If that's what she wants to go by, that's what we'll call her." His deep baritone was just as warm as his smile. Which he aimed at me again. Damn. My chest was going all fluttery. All this hotness in one room was putting me on hormonal overload.

My Disney prince, Aaron, took a careful step toward me. I wasn't sure why Marco had assigned him Doc. Maybe because his bright blue gaze was so thoughtful I almost felt as if he was considering me through a pair of glasses.

"From what Marco's told us, there's a lot you're

unsure of," he said. His voice was even and faintly but pleasantly raspy. "Maybe you could start by telling us what you do know. What has your life been like? What have you been doing with it?"

"I can think of a lot of things *I'd* like to know about now," Kylie mumbled. But somehow having the four guys in the room made me feel more at ease instead of less. I didn't know them—they were total strangers. Why did I feel as if there wasn't anywhere safer in the world I could be than right here with them?

That weird sense of belonging loosened my tongue.

"I've been living here—in New York, I mean—since I was five," I said. "Mostly... Mostly with my mother. It was really just the two of us. She home-schooled me, and we'd go out around the city, but we never really talked to anyone else."

"So you just ate, slept, learned, had a little fun here and there—nothing all that unusual?" Aaron said.

He was fishing for something specific, but I had no idea what. "Nothing except the whole keeping to ourselves part. At least not that I can think of."

"Don't worry about it then." He motioned for me to continue. "But at some point, that changed?"

"Well, like I told Marco, my mom took trips every now and then. When I was fourteen, she left on one, and she didn't come back."

I hesitated, my throat constricting. I'd had seven years to get over that loss, but it still stabbed just as deep. I didn't even know whether to be furious with Mom or to grieve. Had she abandoned me by choice, or had something happened to her out there, wherever she'd gone?

"You've been your own for seven years?" Nate said. He shook his head. "That must have been tough."

I had the urge to go to him and let him wrap those brawny arms around me. But how had he known it'd been seven years since I was fourteen? Had Marco's assistant heard the twenty-first birthday talk in the bar?

"It was okay at first," I said, feeling the need to defend Mom, even though no one had criticized her directly. "My mother owned the apartment we lived in. We had a joint bank account with plenty of savings to cover food and the bills. I could handle myself. But then —the superintendent realized I was living there on my own. He called Child Services and the police. I couldn't stay. They started tracking the bank account, so I had to stop using it."

My voice faded. I looked down at my lap. I didn't want to talk about the rest of it. About the time on the streets, about the allegiances I'd had to form to stay alive. "*That* was tough. That's all you really need to know. But I found my way out. Kylie and I got an apartment of our own last month. I work in a warehouse. I'm good."

My hand had leapt to my necklace of its own accord. My thumb worried the latch, flicking the locket open and closed.

West's jaw twitched. Aaron's gaze jerked to my hand. "That necklace," he said. "Your mother gave that to you?"

"She did. Right before the last time she left." The strangest feeling crept up over me, that I didn't need to tell him I hadn't opened it until yesterday. Something about it—they all already knew.

"Aaron's a bit of a magpie," Marco teased. "An eye for the shinies."

Aaron ignored him. He took another step forward, as if to ask to see it. My fingers closed around the locket. Kylie grasped my other hand, squeezing it reassuringly.

"What *I'd* like to know," West said, his eyes still narrowed, "is what you remember from before you came to New York City."

Before. My pulse lurched, and my mouth went dry. I didn't know why. There was nothing so terrifying about it. Because the truth was: "I don't remember anything." My voice quavered. I paused to steady myself. "I know we moved here from someplace else, but... Everything before is a blank. My mom and I never talked about it."

I'd tried to ask, once, when I was ten. Mom's mouth had gone so tight and tense I'd been ashamed before the question had even finished coming out.

You don't need to think about that, she'd said. *Not for a long, long time.*

"So you haven't got the slightest clue," West started up. Before he could finish his thought, Nate swung around toward him.

"Leave her alone," he growled. "I know you can feel she's telling the truth just as well as I can. Do you really think it's fair to dump everything on her all at once?"

West shut up, but that didn't stop him from glowering at the beefier guy. Marco chuckled, as if he found their squabbling amusing.

"I don't get it," I said, sitting up a little straighter.

"You keep talking as if you know more about this—about me, and my mom—than I do. What's really going on here? Why are you all even *here*?"

And why do you make me feel like I want to somehow jump all of you simultaneously? Yeah, I'd keep that question to myself.

Aaron's tone stayed calm and even. "We knew you a long time ago," he said. "Before you came to the city, when we were all children. The fact that you don't remember... My best guess is that your mother suppressed those memories to make it easier for you not to give yourself away."

"Give *what* away? And what do you mean, 'suppressed'? You're talking like she put a magic spell on me or something."

I laughed a little, but the guys didn't take it as a joke. They exchanged a glance. Aaron ran his hand over his golden-blond hair. "That is one way of putting it."

"Let's just say there's a *lot* your mother didn't tell you." Marco piped up.

Nate shifted toward me. The strong, protective energy of his presence washed over my body, settling my nerves. "There's something you need to know about what we are, and what you are," he said.

"Hold on," West interrupted. "If we have to handle her with kid gloves, fine. But that one doesn't need to hear this. She's got no place in this conversation." He pointed at Kylie.

My fingers tightened around Kylie's. "My best friend stays. That's non-negotiable."

"I don't think you'll get very far arguing the point," Marco said. "I already tried once."

"Yep," Kylie said. "I'm un-budge-able."

West grimaced, but Nate held up his hand. "If Ren trusts her, then we can trust her too. Ren's memory has nothing to do with her emotional awareness."

"It's against policy to break silence with non-kin," Aaron put in. "But I think just this once, we can make a reasonable exception."

"Would you all please stop talking about whether you can say it and get on with it?" I burst out. "What's the big secret? What are 'non-kin'? What the hell—"

I fell silent when Nate moved closer. He sat down on the chair Marco was standing by, kitty-corner around the coffee table from me. The closer he came, the closer I wanted to be to him, but I stayed frozen in place on the settee. His voice came out as warm as before, but his deep brown eyes were so solemn.

"Ren, your mother let you believe that the two of you were just ordinary people. But you're not. And neither are we. We're not human at all. We're shifters."

CHAPTER 5

Ren

For the first few seconds after Nate spoke, I could only gape at him. Finally, I relocated my tongue. "Shifters," I said. "What does that even mean? How am I not human? How are *you* not human? Look at us!"

"That's kind of the point, princess," Marco said lightly. "We *look* human, but when we're in the mood, we can shift. Into something else."

"Something like *what*?"

"Whatever animal essence is tied to your spirit," Aaron said. "It's different for each of us here. But our nature comes with additional powers even when we're in human form. I'm sure you'll have noticed you're stronger, faster, more agile than anyone else in comparable shape, for example."

My heart skipped. I'd become Fisher's best thief because my sticky fingers could snatch a valuable off a person so quickly they'd never notice. The warehouse manager had stared at me when I'd shown him how easily I could handle the heavy boxes. How did Aaron know?

Oh. Because if what he was saying was true, he and the other three guys before me were the exact same way.

"Oh my God!" Kylie said, cocking her head at me. "He's totally right. I know pro athletes who can't move like you do. I always thought it was just cool. But supernatural powers—that totally makes sense." An undercurrent of laughter ran through her words. She didn't totally believe it. She turned to Aaron, her gray eyes sparkling. "Is she supposed to be psychic too? I swear sometimes she knows things about people there's no way she should."

"Ky," I protested, but it was true. I'd known just what soft spot to hit to make that guy in the bar back off. I picked up on the flavor of people's emotions all the time.

"That'll be part of your animal side too," Nate said, but I was too keyed up for even his rich rumble of a voice to be soothing.

Aaron nodded. "Instincts for reading body language, pheromones in the air—our senses extend beyond what any ordinary human would pick up on. And we'd expect you to be particularly sensitive."

I held up my hands. "Okay. So maybe I'm a little weird in a few ways. But I definitely don't have an 'animal side.' I've never 'shifted' into anything. This is the only body I've ever had. I'm pretty sure I'd have noticed if it warped into something completely different."

"Hold up," Kylie said. "I forgot about that part. You shift into *animals*. You're talking, like, werewolves and shit then?" She cracked up, patting my shoulder. "Ren, you're a werewolf! This is awesome."

"Not a werewolf," West muttered where he was still skulking by the door. "Human horror stories have no idea what they're talking about."

"Let's be fair," Marco said. "There are some similarities. But we come in a lot more forms than the garden-variety wolf. And the full moon doesn't really factor in. When we want to shift, we do." He snapped his fingers.

"You know how crazy this sounds, don't you?" I said to all of them. "Again, I repeat, I have never changed into any kind of animal. Not a wolf, not a goldfish, nada."

"There could be a couple of reasons for that," Aaron said. An academic-ish enthusiasm colored his measured voice. He rocked on his heels, looking even more the part of professor—a really, really hot professor. Explaining this stuff was obviously his wheelhouse. "If your memories of knowing you're a shifter have been locked away, you wouldn't have thought to try to exercise those powers. You might have felt an urge, but not known what it meant."

My back stiffened. That clawing sensation that came into my chest when I was caught up in anger—or other sorts of passion. As if there were something inside me trying to dig its way out...

"And," Aaron went on, "none of us come into our full powers until we turn twenty-one. Even if you'd been fully aware of who and what you are, the shift would have taken more effort and been difficult to hold for very long. So it makes sense that it wouldn't have happened automatically."

Nate leaned forward and set his large hand on the side of the settee, just inches from my arm. "Before she left, did your mother tell you anything about your twenty-first birthday? We found you because of a pulse of her magic we started sensing yesterday. I think she must have wanted you to return to your kind."

Kylie's eyes widened. "Your necklace."

I clutched the locket. "She gave me this right before she left. And told me not to open the locket until that birthday. You're saying *it's* some kind of magic?" After everything else they'd already said, that part no longer sounded particularly absurd. Well, actually, it all sounded equally absurd.

West must have heard the incredulity in my tone, maybe because he was so well versed in skepticism himself. "We're all here, aren't we?" he said. "Believe me, it'd have been a lot simpler if we'd found you earlier."

"No." I shook my head. "This is still crazy. Something weird is going on. I'll give you that. But people don't just change into animals. My mom wasn't some kind of witch."

Kylie glanced from one guy to the next, kicking her legs against the base of the settee. "It'd be pretty easy for you to prove it if what you're saying is true, wouldn't it? You said you don't need a full moon. Great! Let's have a shifter demonstration, right here, right now. Your eager audience is waiting." She smiled at them.

Aaron hesitated. "We don't generally reveal ourselves outside our kind."

I waved off his objection. "Oh, please. If you're telling the truth, you've already 'revealed' it. At least if Kylie's here, I can be sure I'm not hallucinating." Except there was such a thing as a group hallucination, wasn't there? Well, I could worry about that if these guys really did start morphing into animals in front of us.

"I'll do it," Nate said, standing up. "How else is she going to believe us?"

He pulled off his cotton tee, revealing a chest even more densely muscled than I'd imagined. Then he reached for the fly of his jeans. My jaw just about dropped to the floor.

"Oh. Um..." Heat flared across my face as Nate shucked off his pants.

Marco chuckled. "You'll find shifters don't have the same hang-ups about getting naked as your average human being. It comes with the territory."

The substantial bulge in Nate's boxers gave me a clear preview of the territory to come. I averted my eyes. I'd never seen a guy naked, not right in front of me. Not some stranger I'd only just met.

Kylie didn't have the same qualms. "You're missing the best part of the show, Ren!" she said, watching avidly. Then her expression froze. Her voice came out thin and tinny. "Holy shit."

My head jerked back around. I wouldn't have thought my jaw could go any more slack, but it did.

Before our eyes, Nate's body was... shifting. There really wasn't a better word for it. The rich brown hair on his head was rippling down to cover all of him in a thick pelt. His torso expanded, his haunches and neck thickening. His face had already lengthened with a narrow snout.

The entire transformation finished moving through his body in the time it took me to blink. I might have thought that kind of bodily change would have to be painful, but it had looked completely natural. Almost... beautiful. A twinge of longing shot through me from collarbone to gut.

Longing and recognition. Yes, that was what people like them were meant to do.

People like *us*.

And now a majestic grizzly bear loomed on its hind legs before me. Its head nearly brushed the light fixture overhead.

No, not *it—him*. Even as my pulse skittered, I knew it was Nate. He lowered himself onto his front legs so that we were at eye level. His deep brown gaze felt just the same as when it had looked at me from his rugged human face. Warm. Protective. The sense of recognition in my gut tugged me toward him. I raised my hand, my fingers curled and then extending.

The bear took a careful step toward me, dipping his head so I could touch the fur between his rounded ears. It was coarse but pleasantly thick to the touch. I had the sudden urge to bury my face in his neck, to drink in the sensation and the musky, peppery smell of him. To feel his protective warmth all around me.

He was a massive predator, but he would never hurt me. He would never let anyone else hurt me either. I knew that, as surely as I'd known the asshole in the bar last night was sore about his ex.

"There," West said. "You've gotten your demonstration."

"This is—" Kylie giggled, a little hysterically. I'd never seen her at a loss for words before. She opened and closed her mouth a few times before she managed to keep going. "Oh my God. It's real. You really—" She laughed again.

Why wasn't I just as shocked? That first glimpse had startled me, but now all I felt was awe and that deep sense of familiarity.

Maybe I'd known, deep down, that it was true, even when my mind had balked to accept it. I swallowed hard and looked up from Nate to the other guys.

"Nate's a bear. What are the rest of you?"

"Jaguar," Marco said. "Not quite as impressive as Nate in size, but I make up for it in other ways." He smirked.

"I'm an eagle shifter," Aaron said. He glanced at West. When the grouchy guy stayed silent, Aaron added, "And West *is* actually a wolf. Most shifters belong to one of four kin-groups. Canine, feline, avian, and, well, everything else." He gestured to West, Marco, himself, and Nate in turn, with a hint of a smile at the last. "We're the leaders of each of those kin-groups. The alphas, by our usual terminology."

"This is seriously the most amazing thing that has ever happened to me," Kylie said. "So when do we get to see the rest of you 'shift'?"

"I don't perform on command," West snapped. But seeing Nate had been enough. I was convinced. Of everything except the last, most important part. Nate nudged my arm with his muzzle, and I rubbed behind his ears automatically, searching for the courage to ask the question that I already knew would upend my life.

Could it really get that much more upended than it already was? I had to know.

I dragged in a breath. "All right. So we know all about you now. Maybe you can tell me—what am *I*?"

At the look Aaron and Marco exchanged, I braced myself. That didn't seem like a good sign. Marco's lips curved with his crooked grin.

"You, my Princess of Flames, put the rest of us to shame. You're a dragon shifter."

West

THE GIRL STARED at Marco as if she couldn't wrap her head around a single word he'd said. Could she really be this ignorant? How could she have gone sixteen years without ever sensing the power inside her, even if her mother had meddled with her memories? I still found it hard to swallow.

"A *dragon?*" she sputtered. Nate, still in his bear form, shuffled backward as she pushed herself to her feet. "Are you kidding me?"

"As much as I enjoy joking around, at this particular moment I'm being totally serious," Marco said.

Ren—of all the things to be calling herself. It sounded like a fragile little bird—gestured vaguely with her hand. "At least bears and wolves and whatever are *real* animals. Dragons don't even exist."

Her disbelief, acted or real, was damn irritating. I

pushed myself off the doorframe and stalked a few paces toward her. "Look, you asked the question. You got the answer." I let my gaze travel over her slim but toned figure. "Although I've got to agree, right now you look like you have about as much fire in you as a puff of sparks."

She turned to glower at me, and I saw a hint of the power in her then. A flicker behind her bright brown eyes. It lit up every inch of my skin as if I'd been hit by a whole shower of sparks.

Damn it. The only thing more irritating than her bewildered human routine was how strongly my body responded to her no matter what I was thinking. I'd been waiting for her way too long.

But this wasn't how my mate was meant to be. She *was* meant to be powerful, stronger than any of us. Not the type to run away from danger and cower among humans for sixteen years. We hadn't known if there were any dragon shifters left. We hadn't known what might be keeping them away. From the sounds of things, it'd been nothing more than fear.

What had her mother been thinking, throwing her back to us now with no understanding of who she was or the role she was meant to fill?

Ren took a step closer to me, and her smell, sweet as strawberries and cream, wafted over me. Enough to make me half hard. Her expression was anything but sweet. She jabbed her finger at my chest, just shy of grazing the thin fabric of my henley.

"I'm trying my best, okay, tough guy?" she said, her eyes all but blazing now. "Try having your world turned completely upside down in the space of an hour sometime, and see how you handle it."

Technically, my world had been turned upside down in the instant I'd felt that first tingle of dragon magic from afar. But I wasn't going to admit that to her. Especially not while her lips were curling with a hint of a smirk.

"And here's your watch back," she said. The thick metal band dangled from her fingers. What the hell? I glanced down at my wrist—which was in fact now bare. Had she just *stolen* that right off me?

Marco's melodic chuckle rang through the room, his dark blue eyes glinting. "Don't you know better than to poke a dragon?"

I grabbed the watch back from Ren, ignoring him. Feline-kin never knew how to mind their own business.

"*I* didn't even see her pull that off," Aaron said with his scholarly awe. He was probably getting a hard-on just from the chance to talk to a dragon up close instead of relying on all those old records he liked to pour over.

The theft had, maybe, been a tiny bit impressive. I re-fastened the watch around my wrist and eyed Ren. Now that she'd gathered a little more confidence, I could almost imagine a dragon's vitality in her. Her eyes were still shining, the deep brown waves of her hair flowing past her shoulders as if recently whipped by the wind. What kind of a dragon would she make after all?

The need to see it wrenched through me. I folded my arms over my chest. "All right, Sparks. You know a few tricks. You want to find out how real dragons are? Shift right now and you'll know."

Ren

West's dark green eyes flashed in challenge. The bravado I'd managed to call up faltered. "I don't know how. I have no idea about any of this. Haven't you been listening?"

I glanced toward Nate, the only person I'd ever seen "shift," and found he'd transformed back into his human self. He was just pulling up his jeans, his sculpted chest still bare. A fresh wave of heat coursed through me at the sight. But—if that was how you shifted—

My arms rose to hug myself, my fingers curling into the sides of my shirt.

"You wouldn't have to undress," Aaron said gently. "You're unlikely to make a full transition on your first try anyway. And if you're able to"—he tipped his head Marco's way—"I suspect our host has plenty of clothes around the house he could spare."

Marco shrugged. Under the jagged fringe of his black hair, his indigo eyes looked suddenly hungry. They gleamed more deeply than the sapphire stud in his ear. "My kin come and go from here. I keep the rooms well-stocked."

"Okay, okay," I said. "But what do I *do*?"

"Well, first, just in case," Marco said, "I think we should take this little party outside, dragons being the size they tend to be. I'd rather not turn this room into a pile of rubble."

"Fine." I wasn't sure what his neighbors would make of it if I did suddenly turn into a gigantic mythical creature, but I was still finding that possibility hard to believe in the first place.

Kylie sprang to her feet. "I'm not missing this!"

Marco swept through the room. We all tramped out back after him.

The second I stepped into the yard, I understood why he wasn't worried about privacy. The small grassy lawn was framed on all sides by tall pines.

I walked a little farther into the middle of the clearing. The guys spread out in a row to watch, Kylie bobbing on her feet beside them.

"Close your eyes," Aaron said. "Reach inside yourself. Try to feel the essence running through you. The core of your nature. Then grasp hold of it and pull it free. It'll want to come. It'll help you."

West had snorted in the middle of that set of instructions, but as mumbo-jumbo-y as they'd sounded, I thought I knew what Aaron meant. I *had* felt the essence running through me before—the flexing of those internal claws.

Like some kind of beast waiting to get out. But a dragon? Really?

I guessed I was going to find out. I inhaled deeply and closed my eyes like he'd said. There it was, waiting for me. That sharp tingle scraping over my ribs. It did want out. I focused my attention on the sensation. *Tell me what to do. Tell me what you need.*

A quiver tickled through my muscles. They flexed as if trying to open themselves up. My skin felt suddenly tight. The tingling inside swelled, as if to burst free—

And contracted, away from my encouragement. I

frowned, squeezing my eyes tighter shut. *Come on. I know you want this.*

A full-out tremor rippled down my spine. I tried to grasp onto that stirring in my core the way Aaron had suggested, but it slipped right through my fingers.

My shoulders sagged. I wavered on my feet, exhaustion rolling over me. I rubbed my eyes before I opened them. How long had I worked at that for? It hadn't seemed like more than a few minutes, but I felt as if I'd just run a marathon.

The guys were still studying me, West with his usual cynical expression, Aaron looking puzzled, Marco considering, Nate concerned. "Are you all right, Ren?" the bear shifter said.

"Yeah," I said. "Yeah." But my legs were shaky when I took a step back toward them. Kylie dashed to my side. "I don't get it. I *felt* it, but it was like it didn't want to come..."

The furrow on Aaron's brow deepened. "Your mother may have suppressed not just your memories, but your powers as well. To make it less likely they'd emerge unexpectedly. But I can't believe she'd have done anything permanent. She must have left you a way of accessing them again."

"You haven't heard from her at all in those seven years?" West said. "Not even a message?"

I shook my head. "Nothing. I don't even know where she was going. All she gave me was the locket." I opened it up and looked at the flame-like symbol inside. "Does this mean anything to you?"

I held out the locket to show them. The other three

took a quick glance and then looked toward Aaron, who I guessed they deferred to on topics requiring much in the way of research. He peered at the etching, but the confusion on his face didn't lift.

"No," he said. "I'm sorry."

"She wouldn't have put that symbol in the necklace if it wasn't important, would she?" Nate said. "It must be meant to tell us something."

"It could be something she'd hoped the last alphas would have told us." Marco's smile was more like a grimace this time.

"Maybe that's something I can help with," Kylie piped up. "I could take a picture and show it around. Out of all the people I know, there might be someone who recognizes it."

All of the guys looked skeptical at that suggestion, but they didn't know Kylie yet. "Sure," I said. "We might as well try."

I tilted the locket's interior to catch the sunlight so she could snap a picture with her phone. She tucked the phone back in her pocket and raked her fingers into her rumpled neon pink hair. "If I'm going to make the rounds, that means I have to go. Do you want to come with? You know you don't have to stay here with these guys if you're not sure about all this yet."

I wasn't sure about much, but the one thing I did know was that none of these four guys—shifters— however I was supposed to think about them—wanted to hurt me. And suddenly I wasn't so sure about the world beyond this house.

Why had Mom been so afraid? What had she been hiding us from?

I didn't think I wanted to find out on my own. And besides, between my short, drugged sleep last night, all the crazy news that had been heaped on me in the last hour, and my failed attempts at shifting, the only place I wanted to go right now was to a bed.

"I'll be okay here," I said. "There's obviously a lot more I need to learn—and I don't think anyone can help me with *that* except these guys. Text me if you find anything out." I turned to Marco. "I assume you've got my phone around here somewhere."

He snapped his fingers. "I knew I'd forgotten something. I thought it was better if we talked before I handed that over, considering the circumstances."

"Is that what you want to do now?" Nate asked. "To talk more with us? There is a lot more we can tell you."

A pressure was starting to build at the back of my skull. I rubbed my neck. "Actually, I think I'd like a little time to myself, if that's okay. To process everything I've already heard. And maybe to take a nap. Having your world tipped over is kind of exhausting."

"That room upstairs is yours for as long as you want it," Marco said. "I'll get Leonard to grab your phone for you."

As he ducked inside, Kylie enveloped me in a hug. "Promise me you're okay with this," she murmured by my ear.

I smiled tightly. I wasn't exactly *okay*, but that wasn't the fault of anyone here. "I just found out I have super powers," I said. "What's not to like?"

She laughed and gave me one last squeeze. "I'll check in with you soon, whether I've got news or not."

She slipped past the trees around the side of the house. The guys followed me back inside. West drew Aaron aside, muttering something to him I assumed was some new complaint about me. Nate came with me up the staircase. I skimmed my hand over the polished wood of the curving banister. Apparently being a shifter also meant being rich, at least for some people. Or maybe that came with being the "alpha."

"Do you have a place like this?" I asked the bear shifter.

Nate grinned. "Marco and I have pretty different senses of style. And our homes belong more to our position as alpha than to *us*. But I do have a few nice properties I'll be looking forward to showing you."

Upstairs, it took me a few tries before I found the bedroom I'd started this adventure in. I paused by the doorway, my awareness of Nate seeping into my skin. The memory rose up of just how much of himself he'd already shown me, and the warmth turned into heat.

Nate reached out and brushed a stray lock of hair back from my cheek. My heart thumped at his touch. "You'll be all right on your own?" he said.

What exactly was he going to propose if I said no? And did I want him to propose it? For a second, my body blared its answer: absolutely yes.

But I was more than just a body, and my mind was too full to be making any clear decisions right now.

"I will," I said. "Thank you."

He teased his fingers deeper into my hair and tipped

my head toward him as he bowed his own. His lips grazed my forehead, and my breath caught. He stepped back, leaving me more flushed than I'd ever been before. I swallowed hard.

"Take whatever time you need," Nate said. He dipped his head. Marco came up from behind him, holding my phone.

"As promised," Marco said. He handed it to me as Nate ambled to the staircase. "Is there any other way your situation here is lacking?"

"I don't think so," I said. I walked into the room to give it a once-over, and Marco followed me. Well, why shouldn't he? It was his house, and he thought I might have something else to ask for. But his closeness beside me made my breath stutter all over again. Heat licked through my veins.

Dear lord, how could I be this horny—and for four guys all at once? Did shifters always provoke that response in other people? Kylie hadn't seemed anywhere near as affected. Maybe it was just between shifters.

If I was going to just accept that I definitely was one.

"No complaints?" Marco said.

"No," I said honestly. "This is the most gorgeous house I've ever seen."

I turned toward him at the same time, which maybe was a mistake. He smiled his slightly wicked smile, gazing back at me with the hunger I'd noticed earlier. An answering desire unfurled in my gut and tingled lower in my belly.

He raised his hand and traced his lithe fingers along the line of my jaw, tipping my face toward his. His languid voice dropped to a murmur. "And you have the most gorgeous eyes I've ever seen. So brilliant they're more amber than brown. Like fire. A person could fall right into them."

"Falling into fire?" I joked in a half-hearted attempt to diffuse the electricity between us. "That sounds pretty dangerous. You'd want to climb back out fast."

"Maybe not," Marco said. "I suspect it would be a very pleasant burning."

As if drawn up by his words, a rush of heat seared through me. Marco leaned his head a little closer. Before I caught control of myself, I'd pressed my lips to his.

He kissed me back with an encouraging growl. His mouth slid against mine, hot and teasing, coaxing my lips apart. His hand slipped back to tangle in the hair at the base of my neck. Everywhere he touched me, I felt as if I *had* caught on fire.

I gripped his shoulders as if I could pull our mouths even closer together. His tongue caressed mine, and I groaned into him. My hips arched toward his. His other hand trailed down my side, drawing a path of flames through my clothes.

I wanted those clothes off. I wanted him on the bed, over me, inside me. I wanted—

What the *hell* was I doing?

I wrenched myself away from Marco. My body protested so sharply it felt as if I'd literally torn us apart. Marco let his hand drop to his side. He watched me with heavy-lidded eyes, no judgment or accusation in them.

He was a stranger. I'd met him just a few hours ago.

After he'd pretty much had me kidnapped. Obviously all this supernatural talk had addled my brain.

And *I* was the one who'd kissed *him*.

My face flushed again, with embarrassment this time. And maybe some lingering desire. It wasn't as if I'd stopped wanting him just because common sense had kicked in.

"I'm sorry," I said, my voice rough. "I didn't mean to—I don't know if this is normal for shifters, but it's not normal for me."

"You draw the lines, Princess of Flames," he said. "I'm happy to take whatever you feel ready to give, but when you say stop, we stop." He tilted his head toward the bed. "Why don't you get that rest I'm sure you'll need? We've still got a long way to go."

Ren

WE WERE STANDING in a private cabin on a train—my mother and me. The floor hitched under my feet, and the window was rattling. We were racing far, far away. Far from the bad thing that still had my chest twisted tight, even as I tried not to think about it.

My mother knelt down to my eye level and cupped my cheek. Her eyes were wild as a stormy sky.

"Listen to me, Serenity," she said in a choked voice. "Somewhere deep down, where no one else can touch it, you need to remember you're a dragon. *Always* remember."

I blinked at her with a childish confusion. "Of course I'll remember, Mama. I can't *not* be a dragon."

A sad smile curved her lips. "Oh, darling. For a little while, I need you to forget. At least on the surface. But you're right. You'll never not be."

She raised her hands and pressed her palms to my temples. Darkness swirled into my head. The scene pivoted.

I was running with my mother through a forest, her hand clasped tight around mine. So tight it hurt. My breath stung in my throat. My lungs ached. I tripped on a root, and she heaved me up in an instant. We ran and ran and—

I was crouched behind the big vase in the front hall, listening for girlish laughter. My heart thumped giddily. This time I'd be the last one found. This time I'd be the queen of hide-and-seek. They might be older than me, but I—

I was sitting in the grass, sweet clover scent filling my nose, laughter in my throat. A shape streaked by through the clear blue sky above me. Brilliant bronze scales, like her eyes. The flap of massive wings sending a comforting breeze over me. I clapped my hands together.

"Mama!"

My eyes popped open, back in the present. I stared at the wall across from me for a second as the dream faded and the real world came back into focus. Gold flowers winding through mint-green wallpaper. A velvet bedspread tucked under my chin. A sinfully soft mattress cradling my body.

Memories rushed in. Marco's house. The four shifters. Nate transforming into a bear. West's snarking. Aaron's careful explanations. All the things they'd told me. My failed attempt at shifting.

Nate's lips brushing my forehead. Marco's pressed hard against mine.

I sat up in the bed, heat washing over me. Yep, that had all been real. And I was still here.

My gaze shot to the window. The daylight was even paler than it had been in the morning, but it was streaming in at the same angle. As if it were morning again.

God, had I slept through half a day and then the entire night? All those dreams spinning me around...

I paused, my fingers curling into the bedspread. No, those hadn't been just dreams, had they? I felt the truth of them like an ache in the base of my throat. Those had been as real as those room. Real memories, from when I was a little girl. From before Mom and I had come to the city.

From when I'd known I was a dragon. When I'd seen her, soaring above me, like she was meant to.

The four alphas had been telling the truth. Mom had locked away my memories. She'd practically admitted to me she was going to do it before she had.

I was a dragon. I was a *dragon*.

I looked down at my hands, as if they might have sprouted scales and talons. Nope, those still looked like perfectly normal human fingers.

Had I ever shifted myself? I couldn't remember. Couldn't dredge up any fragments of my past other than the ones that had floated into my dreams. Aaron had suggested it'd have been more difficult when I was younger, and I'd only been five when Mom had locked those parts of me away.

Why had she done that? Why couldn't she have

trusted me? At least before she'd wandered off wherever she'd gone...

Anger hit me, biting into my chest. But another ache closed around it. I missed her. So goddamn much. Not just the Mom I remembered clearly, either. The one I'd glimpsed, wild and powerful and more than human.

Was I ever going to get her back?

That question felt too big to sit with on my own. Especially when I'd apparently wasted half a day recovering from yesterday's revelations. I crawled out of the bed, stretched, and looked down at myself. I'd been wearing this tee and jeans for almost two days now. They were getting a little grimy feeling.

Marco had commented that he had lots of spare clothes around. I eased open the drawers of the dresser and found one full of lady-type clothing, although fancier than the stuff I'd normally have put on. I settled on a silky violet blouse and decided my jeans could hold up to another wearing as long as I got the rest of myself clean.

I'd seen a bathroom while searching for this bedroom yesterday. I crept down the hall and ducked inside. To my relief, there was a lock on the inside knob.

Tension seeped out of me as the shower streamed into my hair and down my back. I rubbed my hands over my body, letting the hot water carry away two days of sweat and uncertainty.

I was a dragon shifter. I still didn't totally understand what that entailed, but there were four guys waiting here in the house to help me figure it out. I was ready.

I dried myself with a towel so fluffy I was tempted to bury myself in it and never come out. The silk shirt clung to my figure a little more than I liked, but at least the scooped neckline showed minimal cleavage. I was having enough trouble keeping my hands off of Marco—and, let's be real, Nate too—without wearing clothes that screamed *Do me.*

Combing my fingers through my still-damp hair, I padded down the staircase to the first floor. A buttery smell was wafting from what I assumed was the direction of the kitchen.

Hunger twanged through my stomach. My last meal of sausage and eggs might as well have been a year ago. My feet pushed me faster of their own accord. I dashed around the bend in the staircase and careened over the edge of the next step.

Anyone looking on would have thought I'd slipped and fallen. I guessed I sort of had. But the tumble gave me a jolt of excitement, not fear. I opened my arms as if to embrace the sensation—and brought them down to help me catch my landing at the base of the stairs. My knee jarred against the floor with a thump, but I hardly felt the impact. My spirit was still soaring.

Like the dragon in my memory. The dragon who'd been my mother.

Was that why I got off so much on jumps and falls? I'd always thought it was some random daredevil impulse, but maybe I simply missed the feeling of flight. Some part of me deep down had never completely forgotten it.

A figure appeared in the hall. Stocky, muscular, with a golden shine in his pale hair—Aaron. He was wearing a linen tunic with a slit neck that gave a glimpse of his impressive tanned chest. His expression relaxed when he saw me straightening up.

"I heard a thud," he said. "Did you fall down?"

I shrugged, smiling at him. I hadn't talked one-on-one with Aaron yet, but I appreciated the thoughtful approach he'd taken to my situation. Out of the four alphas who'd come to find me, he was the only one who didn't seem to have any specific expectations of who I'd be or what I'd do. He preferred to observe who I actually was.

"I've had worse," I said. I nodded to the spatula in his hand. "Are you the one cooking?"

He smiled back. "Hungry? No one's up yet, not even Marco's chef. I didn't want to hassle anyone else on my behalf. Most shifters are more on the nocturnal side, but I'm a bit of an early bird." His grin widened as if daring me to laugh.

"Ha, ha, Mr. Eagle. I just hope you're not cooking eggs."

He brandished the spatula. "Pancakes. Come on. I'd better get back to them before they burn."

"I definitely cannot be responsible for massacring your pancakes."

I followed Aaron into the kitchen. He strode straight to the stove where a huge frying pan was sizzling and grabbed another plate from a cupboard. I stopped on the threshold, gaping.

"Wow." The kitchen was as big as the entire open-concept common space in the apartment I was sharing with Kylie, with stainless steel appliances as far as the eye could see. "Now that's a kitchen."

"I don't think Marco knows how to do anything halfway," Aaron said. "It's all-out-luxury, or forget about it." He flipped the pancakes, sending a fresh waft of that buttery doughy smell to my nose.

My mouth started watering. I ambled up beside him to check whether his handiwork was close to done.

Aaron looked over at me. "Are you feeling more settled now that you've had time to think all this through?" His voice came out a little softer than usual, but still with that appealing rasp. My awareness of his presence snapped into focus with a warmth all down my side. We were standing close enough that I could smell him, a salty aquatic scent that reminded me of the ocean. I wanted to lick it off his skin.

Down, girl. Mind out of the gutter.

"Yeah," I said, my throat suddenly hoarse. Why did *every* one of these guys have this effect on me? "I guess I was kind of a pain in the ass yesterday, huh?"

Aaron chuckled. "Not at all. It was totally understandable. I like a girl who wants all the facts instead of just accepting whatever she's told."

So he liked *me* then? Oh, why did I even care? But I did. There I was peeking at him through my eyelashes while I tried to figure out the best response to make him laugh again.

"I like a man who has all the facts," I settled on.

That got me a grin. I'd take it. "Maybe not all of them," Aaron said. "But I do like to learn as much as I can about our people and our history. The way I see it, the only way you can avoid future mistakes is if you understand your past."

A sound theory. "That gets harder when you don't even remember your past," I muttered.

"I have to think those memories will start to come back now that you're back in the fold, so to speak. Your mother wouldn't have wanted you to be cut off from your powers permanently. She must have expected that we'd help you recover them."

He tossed the pancakes onto the waiting plates, two each, and drizzled them with maple syrup. My hands snatched up the first plate when he offered it to me, but there was one question I had to ask before I stuffed anything in my mouth.

"I still don't understand—how *did* my mother let you know to find me? I get that it had something to do with the locket, but other than that..."

Aaron led me out of the kitchen into a dining room that was way too big for the two of us. Fourteen chairs stood around a massive rosewood table. Aaron set his plate down at the foot of the table, but he turned to me instead of sitting. I put down my plate too and leaned my elbow on the top of the chair beside me, waiting for his answer.

"When we're named alpha, there's a full ceremony involved." Aaron held out his left hand, palm up, revealing a scar like a sunburst of lines in the middle of his palm. "This mark ties us to our kin-group, and to the dragons. The moment you opened that locket, whatever magic your mother worked on it activated. I felt it right there, in the middle of my hand, with a sense of direction. But I'd guess any shifter who was closer enough would have been able to feel it. From what I understand, that's how Marco sent his lieutenant ahead to track you down."

This time, I let my impulses take over. I took Aaron's hand in both of mine. "May I?" I said, abruptly breathless. He nodded, his clear blue eyes fixed on my face. I felt it then, with the thump of my pulse.

He might not *expect* anything from me, but he wanted things. The same kinds of things I found myself wanting when we stood this close together.

I dragged my gaze away from his to his palm. My thumb skimmed across it to trace the lines of his scar. He held still, but the muscles in his arm flexed. The breath he took sounded slightly ragged. I wondered how he'd react if I kissed that spot. Just the thought sent a pulse of heat between my legs.

I swallowed hard and yanked my mind back to our conversation. There was something he'd said...

"You said this mark ties you specifically to the dragons," I said. "Why? I mean, shouldn't we have our own alpha or something? Where *are* the other dragon shifters?" My heart leapt with a sudden hope. Did I have other family—grandparents or cousins or who knew what —that Mom and I had left behind?

Aaron turned his palm over, engulfing my slender hand in his larger one. He traced his thumb over the delicate skin on the back, sending a pleasant shiver up my arm.

"Dragons have always been the rarest of the shifters, as well as the most powerful," he said, even more quietly than before. Almost reverent. "To the best of our knowledge right now, you might be the last one."

"The *last?*" I repeated. The words struck a chord in me, but it was hard to think clearly with his careful thumb sliding back and forth over my skin.

Aaron nodded. "Which is why it was so important to your mother that she protect you. As long as shifters have walked this earth, the dragons among us have played a special role, one no one else can fill."

"Great. No pressure there." My laugh came out shaky. "So what exactly does that mean?"

The corner of his lips curled up. "The dragon shifters are the core of all shifter-kind. They unite the kin-groups with one common tie, by taking all four alphas as their mates."

CHAPTER 8

Ren

Aaron's last comment was not the kind of revelation anyone should drop on a girl before she's even had breakfast. I stared at him, my fingers closing around his to stop the caress of his thumb—but not letting go. Because even as the shock rippled through me, some part of me leapt to accept the idea.

Yes. They were *mine*, all of them.

I shook that thought away. "Hold on. Just so I'm clear, you're saying that if I'm the last dragon shifter there is, my 'role' is to hook up with the four of you alphas?"

The corner of Aaron's lips crooked up. "Not just 'hook up with.' The mate-bonds shifters form are lifelong. You'd be partnered with all of us, 'til death do us part."

"That seems kind of... greedy, grabbing the four most important"—and hottest, I added silently—"guys around."

"Like I said, it's considered right because it unites the four kin-groups. I've looked back through the old records, as far back as shifters have kept them, and from what I've seen, our community has always worked that way. It's so natural it's woven into our beings."

He paused, studying my expression. His voice dropped to a pitch that sent eager shivers over my skin. "You've felt it, haven't you? That pull toward each of us—the same way we all feel toward you."

My breath caught. I couldn't look away from his brilliant blue eyes. I wet my lips, and his gaze dropped to them. Suddenly they felt as hot as if he'd already kissed them.

How could I lie to him when he was looking at me like that?

"I have felt it," I said. My voice came out in a murmur.

"Then you understand how innate it is. How meant-to-be."

He raised my hand to press a kiss to my knuckles. The heat of that touch flared down my arm and right through the core of me. I might have yanked him into a different sort of kiss if someone hadn't cleared his throat rather rudely at that exact moment.

I flinched back from Aaron, an embarrassed flush prickling over me. West was standing in the kitchen doorway, his arms crossed in his usual standoffish pose. His dark green eyes glowered at us.

"That might be how it's worked before, but that doesn't mean it's supposed to stay that way forever," he said in his low, throaty voice.

Aaron rested his hand reassuringly on the small of my back. My embarrassment didn't stop me from wanting to lean into him.

But the most infuriating thing was that neither that embarrassment nor West's jerk-ish demeanor stopped the pull drawing me toward the wolf shifter too. Even as I glared back at him, some part of me longed to see that handsome face soften with affection. A few strands of his silvery auburn hair had drifted across his angular cheekbones, and my hand itched to tuck it behind his ear. To linger on his cheek afterward.

I curled my fingers into my palm. Meant to be or not, West clearly wasn't mooning over me.

"We've got more reason to believe the arrangement should stay the same than that it should change," Aaron said. "That pattern of stability has held the kin-groups in balance for hundreds if not thousands of years."

"How do we know it's the arrangement that's kept us in balance?" West said. "Maybe we'd have been just fine without it too."

Aaron's mouth tightened. "That's a careless perspective to take. Throwing aside all that history could ruin us. Look at how things have gone even in sixteen years without the dragons present."

West shrugged. "Because we've been waiting and waffling, not knowing what to do, not letting ourselves make any decisions. Maybe it's time. Maybe all it'd take is for us to step up and pick a different path."

I didn't feel enough connection to these politics to try to argue on either side. And anyway, my mind had kept spinning with Aaron's revelation, which was bringing up all sorts of other questions.

"Wait," I said. "If this is how it always worked, with the dragon shifters and the alphas... My mother must have had four mates, right? One of them would be my father. Is he still—do you know who he is?"

I tried to keep my hopes in check, but excitement bubbled up inside me. Mom had never been willing to say much on the subject of my father, but I'd always wondered. Especially in the seven years since she'd left.

Then I noticed how West's expression had tensed. Aaron looped his hand right around my waist. "Every dragon shifter has four fathers," he said. "That's part of the unique structure of our rulership. A dragon can only be formed from the best qualities of all four kin-alphas: the loyalty of the wolves, the strength of the bears, the cunning of the wildcats, and the grace of the birds of prey. When all is at harmony between a dragon and her mates, a new dragon may be conceived."

I blinked. "*Four* dads." But the solemn note in his voice hadn't escaped me either. "What happened to them?"

He swallowed audibly. "The alphas before us, the ones who were your mother's mates, they passed away— passing on the responsibility to us... right before she left."

I turned to look him in the face. "Sixteen years ago? You must have been awfully young."

He waved aside my concern with the hand not resting on my waist. "Marco was ten, West and me eleven, and Nate twelve. Old enough that our mentors knew we'd grow into the roles. Every alpha has trusted advisors—the ones already in place worked alongside us almost like regents until we were of age to hold our own."

So they grew up like that, one generation after the next, dragons and alphas in unison. "You don't pass being alpha on to your kids," I said slowly, piecing what he'd said together. "I'm assuming? Do the alphas *only* mate with a dragon shifter—and only one? All of your kids would be dragon shifters, then?"

"And only one quarter ours," West put in from behind me.

Aaron frowned at him. "It isn't that less of us goes into helping make a dragon than any other child. It's that a dragon child is so much more than any other." He turned his attention back to me. "You're right, we don't pass on rule from parent to child, at least not that way. The alphas before us were your fathers. They picked us from the kin-group because they believed we'd be strong leaders—and the best mates for their daughter."

I didn't know how I felt about that. A few minutes ago, I hadn't known anything about my dad—or dads. I wasn't ready for them to suddenly be picking out my future partners-for-life.

"So the *daughters* never have any say in it?"

The corner of Aaron's lips twitched, I thought with amusement. "Oh, you can have a say. If a dragon feels one or more of her offered mates is unsuitable, she can reject him and wait for the kin-group to propose another. Or... Another shifter can fight to take the role of alpha from the one chosen. If the chosen alpha isn't strong enough to fend off the attack, then they weren't worthy of the honor anyway."

"Is that what happened to the alphas before you?" I said, and then realized that didn't make sense. If the previous alphas had been challenged and lost, then presumably the disciples they'd chosen would've been chucked aside as well. What the hell could have happened to all four of the last guys, all at once?

"No," Aaron said. His expression shuttered. "That was a more complicated situation. I think it'd be better if we waited to discuss that once more of your memories have returned."

He obviously took me for a much more patient person than I was. I opened my mouth to push for answers, but West raised his voice at the same moment.

"None of that matters anyway. Those decisions belonged to the old alphas—the ones before us and the ones before them. We're in charge now. We can make up our own minds about how we do things. And that includes whether we *do* you."

The edge in his voice made me grit my teeth. Some mate he was turning out to be. I swiveled around, my eyes narrowing. "Is that how you show the wolf 'loyalty' you're supposed to be known for?"

My jab hit the mark. I could tell from the way his shoulders stiffened. But his voice was firm when he bit out his reply.

"One more on the long list of things you need to learn, Sparks: Loyalty given blindly is worthless. I'm loyal first and always to my kin. To you? I haven't seen any reason to be so far."

"Well, you're not exactly inspiring a whole lot of confidence so far either," I snapped back.

"All right." Aaron held up his hands in a gesture for peace. "Let's table this discussion, all right? This is a strange situation for all of us. We've got a lot more getting to know each other to do before anyone decides anything."

He squeezed my shoulder. "Which is why I've been thinking we should see what we can do about activating your powers. Maybe once you have more of your dragon senses at your disposal, you'll find it easier to follow the path your mother seems to have left for you."

I jerked my gaze away from West's, willing my shoulders to come down from around my ears. "Okay. Something to actually *do* sounds good to me."

"Good. We'll eat, and then we'll see what we can unearth in there."

His smile settled my nerves a little. But as I pulled out my chair to sit down, the pancake smell trickling into my nose again, something else he'd said earlier twisted around my gut.

You might be the last one.

The last of the dragon shifters. That could only be true if Mom was no longer around. I'd known there might be a permanent reason she couldn't come back, but I'd never let myself follow that line of thought very far. The alphas had clearly thought it, though.

Maybe she hadn't come back because she was dead. Because something, wherever she'd gone, had killed her.

CHAPTER 9

Aaron

THE MUSCLES in Serenity's back flexed under my pressing fingers. I eased my hands in a slow line between her shoulder blades, fighting to focus only on the task at hand and not how much I wanted to touch every other part of her as well. She felt like a live wire beneath her silk shirt. So much power bottled in that slim frame. It was breathtaking.

"Picture the wings waiting there, folded tight, longing to unfurl," I said, keeping my voice quiet and even. I thought of the sensations my own body went through, as the only alpha who knew what it was like to transform into a winged creature. "Immerse yourself in that sensation. Send them the strength they need to break through."

My dragon shifter grimaced where she was kneeling on the back lawn. Her pale fingers had dug into the long grass. The rising summer sun was baking the yard, creating a warm green smell that mingled with the tartly sweet scent of her body.

"I'm trying," she said. "I'm trying everything you're saying. It just doesn't want to come." She let out a sound of frustration.

I couldn't imagine what it was like, having so much power coursing through your veins and not being able to release it. Maybe I was pushing her too hard. The thought made my chest constrict. At least West hadn't followed us outside. His constant criticism couldn't be helping things.

"Hey," I said. I sat down on the grass beside Serenity and slid my fingers up her jaw to turn her face toward me. She looked back at me, frustration shimmering in her amber eyes. Frustration and a heat that deepened when I let my thumb graze her cheek.

God, how could I not answer that longing? The same heat coursed through me. "It'll be okay," I told her. "You've got a lot of years of lost practice to make up for. It'll come."

Then I leaned in and kissed her.

I let my lips brush hers lightly at first. She'd only just found out the full truth about our connection. She hadn't seemed unwilling, but she hadn't leapt for joy either. It might be too soon.

No. She leaned into me, pressing her mouth harder against mine. The heat I'd felt before flared through me.

This was her. My dragon, my mate. I hadn't known for sure I'd ever get the chance to meet her, let alone get this close to her. Every inch of me, including the length hardening in my pants, clamored to make that true in every meaning of the word.

I tugged her a little closer, angling my lips in a way that drew a gasp from hers. I wasn't going to make a spectacle of us here on Marco's lawn, even though we were alone for the moment, but I wasn't going to let the other three get in the way of this partnership either. They could grumble or preen or hang back in chivalry all they wanted. Serenity needed a mate who was here for her right now, in every way she needed.

I'd never wanted anything more than to be that man.

Apparently I was making a spectacle of us despite my best intentions. The back door whispered open. Before I'd found the will to draw back from the kiss, Marco's familiar chuckle carried across the lawn.

"I'm thinking we need a recap on the differences between training and making out."

I eased away, tipping my forehead against Serenity's just for a moment. She sighed with what sounded like regret. We both looked up to see the other three alphas standing in a line.

"Sometimes a little of the latter can help guide the former," I said lightly, standing up.

Ren

I pushed myself onto my feet and gazed back at the assembled alphas. This time, only a flicker of embarrassment warmed my cheeks.

Why shouldn't I be kissing Aaron? Why shouldn't the rest of them see it? I was supposed to be kissing *all* of them at some point or another, from what he'd said. It was practically fated.

Apparently all I needed was one tiny excuse and I turned into a total exhibitionist. Who would have guessed? Not any of my ex-attempted-flings, that was for sure.

"If you've got some better idea for unlocking the dragon in there," I said, tapping my head, "I'm all ears."

Nate cocked his head, his expression pensive. I couldn't look at him without picturing the huge bear that had stood in his place for a little while yesterday. His chestnut hair gleamed exactly the same shade. But the way he'd behaved toward me so far had been more teddy bear than predator.

"If Aaron's strategies aren't working, I'm not sure any of us could come up with something better," he said. "But if there's anything you need me to do, just say so."

"Maybe we should leave the shifting aside for now and find out where we can get with the powers she's already showing," West said, with a skeptical glance over my body. "I'd like to see what she can do."

And what I couldn't, his tone implied.

I raised my chin. "Fine by me. Where do we start?"

"What were those qualities you mentioned?" West said, glancing at Aaron. "Speed, agility, and strength? Speed seems like an easy place to start."

"She's not really dressed for working out," Nate said.

"She's not going to get to call a time-out and go change every time she has to act."

I brushed my hands over the silky violet shirt. I'd worn jeans through most of my exploits in the city. They felt perfectly comfortable. The blouse was light and flexible enough, just fancier than I usually bothered with. "As long as Marco doesn't mind me possibly ruining his nice clothes, I'm good to go."

Marco smirked. "There's plenty to go around. I'm looking forward to seeing you in action, princess."

"We can start simple," West said, as if I needed coddling. "How fast can you run from one side of the yard to the other?"

"Faster than you, maybe," I said, but he glowered at me rather than responding to the challenge. I shrugged and ambled over to the line of trees that bordered the yard.

"You don't have to go along with this," Nate said.

"It's fine." I smiled at them all, with a little extra sharpness for West. "If it shuts him up for a few minutes, it's a win all around."

Marco raised his hand to his mouth as if trying to hold in his snicker—and failing. West turned his glare on the jaguar shifter. Marco just raised an eyebrow. "You asked for this."

"It *would* probably be useful for us to know exactly where your abilities are at," Aaron said calmly. "Are you ready?"

"On your marks, get set, go," I said, and pushed my feet off the lawn's spongy ground. I dashed for the stretch of trees across from me, pushing all my energy into my legs, as if there was a police officer chasing after me. Or a mark who'd caught on to a theft. Or some guy who really didn't want to take no as an answer.

All situations I'd experienced at least once.

My feet pounded the grass. The warming air rushed past me. I burst past the first few trees and caught myself, spinning around. A grin split my face. That had been kind of fun.

I walked back to the edge of the lawn, wiping my hands together. "All right, what've you got next?"

I must have done all right. Marco, Aaron, and Nate all looked pleased in their own ways. And West looked pissed, which meant I'd performed better than he liked. I gave him a pointed glance. I hadn't even broken a sweat yet.

"How long can you keep that up for?" he said. "A thirty-foot dash is nothing. You need endurance too."

"Do you have a longer track for me to take on?" I said. "Or are you suggesting I just run back and forth like a crazy person?"

He gave me a thin smile. "You'd better make do with what we have."

Oh, he'd like it if I backed down, wouldn't he? As if I hadn't been in situations ten times more humiliating than this in the last seven years. He had no idea what "endurance" meant. I wasn't going to let his arrogance get to me.

"No problem," I said, keeping my tone breezy. "I wouldn't mind giving my legs a good stretch anyway."

I took off without any preamble this time. I raced across the lawn to my starting point, pivoted on my feet, and zipped back the way I'd come. Once I fell into the rhythm of the thump of my feet and the heave of my breaths, the growing burn in my muscles was almost pleasant. I gave myself over to the sensation, not bothering to count repetitions. Just flying back and forth over the yard as if, if I pushed myself a tiny bit farther, I might actually leave the ground.

I had worked up a bit of a sweat, slick under the silky shirt, when West leapt forward in the middle of one of my dashes. He swung out his foot as if to trip me. But my instincts had taken over the second I'd seen him moving. I was already dodging out of the way. I slowed and swiveled, folding my arms over my chest.

"Really?"

"We're supposed to be testing agility too," he said, looking not even slightly guilty.

"And she's having no problem showing you up in that area too," Marco said.

"We're not done yet." West pointed to one of the tallest trees at the back of the yard. "How high can you climb?"

His smirk had come back. Probably thinking that in the city I hadn't gotten much experience with trees. And maybe I hadn't, but there'd been plenty of fences and buildings to clamber up.

"Would the top work for you?" I asked.

I marched over to the tree without waiting for an answer. All I got was an inarticulate mutter anyway.

The pine's lowest branches jutted from its narrow trunk about a foot over my head. Low enough that I could still reach them with my arms extended, but I bent my knees and sprang up so I could hook my elbow right over one. Hugging it, I walked my feet up the trunk until I could swing my legs over the branch too. Then I scrambled up and reached for the next one.

Once I was in the tree, climbing was way easier than West must have realized. The branches were spaced so close together it was more like hefting myself up a ladder than any real challenge. I pulled myself along as quickly as I could without completely losing my breath. Sap was smearing the violet fabric of the shirt, but Marco had said not to worry about that. The pungent pine smell filled my nose. I drank it in with another grin.

As I got higher up, the branches grew thinner. So did the trunk. A hot breeze whipped past me, making the upper half of the tree sway. I gripped the rough bark tighter and kept going.

When my climbing material had pretty much run out, several feet from the tree's peak, I wrapped one arm around the trunk and glanced down. I'd come a little higher than the roof of Marco's house. In the yard below, Nate raised his hand to give me a thumbs-up. I couldn't see West's expression, but I'd bet it was even grouchier than usual.

And I could make him even more peeved. My grin widened as the urge came over me. The fall was twice my leap from the bedroom window yesterday, but a little extra risk just made it more exhilarating.

I stepped forward on the branch and jumped.

The air whistled past my ears. The blouse's sleeves billowed around my arms. For a second, I could imagine the wind catching them, lifting me up to soar toward the sky. My breath caught with a knot of longing beneath my sternum.

Someone let out a worried shout. Then I was hitting the ground, balls of my feet first. Pushing off them, I bent my knees into a roll. I tumbled over on my shoulder and flipped back onto my feet, straightening up in one smooth motion. My feet stung a little and my breath was still ragged, but damn, that had been a delicious sensation.

Aaron was giving me his usual quiet smile. "It looks to me like agility isn't a concern. And I think between all those tests, we've also covered strength pretty well."

West's jaw had clenched. Something flickered in his eyes, an emotion I couldn't quite put my finger on until he opened his mouth.

"In the real world, we don't pull stupid stunts like that unless our lives depend on it."

His tone was snarky, but my ears picked up a faint tremor underneath. I paused with a retort on my tongue.

He'd been a little scared for me, despite himself. And he hated that, didn't he? Hated it so much he needed me to snark back at him so he could go back to being pissed off with me.

Too bad. I wasn't going to give him what he wanted. I'd give him the exact opposite.

"I'm not going to argue with you about it," I said, keeping my voice soft and even. "You've got to trust I don't take risks without knowing what I can handle. And if you need to find some new reason to be angry with me, you'll have to come up with it on your own instead of trying to pick a fight."

West's lean body tensed. "Don't start thinking you

can read people's minds, Sparks," he said, but he looked more unsettled than angry.

Nate rested his large hand on my shoulder. "Dragons see more than any of the rest of us can," he said approvingly.

I rubbed the back of my neck. I'd enjoyed the physical exertion while I was in the middle of it, but the effort was starting to catch up with me. Especially after all those failed attempts at shifting beforehand.

Sure I was quick and strong, and I could take a stab at people's emotions when I needed to. What good was any of that to the alphas if I couldn't make the full transformation into a dragon? I still didn't have a clue what Mom had been trying to tell me with the symbol in my locket.

How long would these guys stick with me before they gave up and—

A jolt of panic shot through me. I clamped down on that thought before my mind could finish it and pushed it away.

"I think our Princess of Flames has more than proven herself for the morning," Marco's smooth voice broke in. "As host to this party, I say we give her a break." He held out his hand to me with his crooked smile. Even with me tired and uncertain, it still provoked a flutter of attraction in my chest.

"There are a few parts of this house you haven't seen yet," he said. "One in particular I think you'll appreciate. Are you up for a quick tour?"

CHAPTER 10

Ren

As soon as I stepped into the house with just Marco beside me, a weight seemed to lift off my shoulders. All the pressure of having the four guys watching me, thinking about me... and me thinking about *them*. Some part of me might like the idea that they were all meant to be with me, but the feeling was still overwhelming sometimes.

How had Mom gone from that to having no male companionship at all for all those years, without ever showing she missed it? She must have. Maybe she'd just been too good at hiding it for me to notice.

Leonard was in the main hall, dusting the frame of an oil painting hanging on the wall. So Marco really had put his lieutenant on cleaning duty. Marco shooed him away, I guessed realizing I still might not be feeling super friendly toward the guy who'd grabbed me in the bar. That was fine with me.

"So what's this part of the house you're so eager to show off?" I asked Marco.

"You'll see." He guided me past the kitchen and down a hall toward the south side of the house with a hand on my back. The light contact sent a pulse of heat over my skin. My thoughts slipped back to yesterday. To that kiss in the bedroom. Just remembering it made my entire body flush.

Was the pull between us always going to feel this intense? Or did it ease off a little once the guys and I were officially mates? I had no idea how a relationship like that worked. But asking Marco directly felt way too awkward. He could probably already tell how much his presence affected me. The last thing I wanted to discuss with him was my out-of-control horniness.

"Here we are." He pushed open a door and ushered me through. The second I stepped inside, my jaw dropped. All thoughts of horniness went temporarily out the window.

Or windows, maybe would be more accurate. The room we'd stepped into was walled on three sides by enormous panes, like a massive greenhouse attached to the side of the house. The late morning sunlight streamed in from between the trees outside, warming the place with a comfortable glow. The floor space wasn't huge, maybe ten feet by ten, but the walls rose at least two stories into the air. Ledges and outcroppings in the shape of thick branches protruded from the walls at varying intervals. It was like looking up into a tiered jungle canopy.

"This house is a way station for any of my kin traveling through these parts," Marco said, looking pleased with my awed reaction. "There's not much room to run around in shifted form outside. This gives us a place to exercise our feline selves in privacy."

It was easy to imagine tigers and leopards—and jaguars—leaping from branch to branch or sunning themselves on one of those ledges. But all those windows... The trees didn't appear to provide total shelter. "Aren't you worried about someone wandering by and seeing you?"

Marco motioned to the walls. "That's one-way glass. On the outside, it's blank. We can see out, but no one can see in. We can get up to whatever we want without worrying about prying eyes." He arched a teasing eyebrow at me. The one with the scar through it.

How had he gotten that wound? A scuffle with another shifter? Or some other conflict I wouldn't have understood yet?

"Is it normal for shifters to live this close to a big city like New York?" I asked. "You must have to be really careful, even with a house like this."

Marco shook his head. "Maybe it's feline obstinacy, but my kin don't play so well by the rules. In theory, most of the country is divided up between the dominant supernatural groups. The cities are vampire territory, because they find it easiest to blend in—and they need a large supply of people to pick from for feeding." He grimaced. "Shifters mostly stick to small towns and countryside, the middle-ground between civilization and wilderness. But my kin's alphas have always liked to keep an eye on what's going on even in the places we're not supposed to be."

My eyes had widened. "Wait. There are *vampires* too? Living in New York?"

"Not a lot of them," Marco said, but his tone had turned more serious. "They like to keep their community rather... exclusive. But there are still more than enough of the bloodsuckers. If you're lucky, you'll never have to deal with them." He shuddered, and then gave me a more typical smile. "So let's not spend any more time talking about them. How would you like a proper climb?"

Now that I'd accepted the existence of shifters, my brain had obviously recalibrated its threshold for belief. If werewolves—and werebears and werejaguars and so on—existed, why the hell not vampires?

I looked up at the jungle gym above me, and my earlier fatigue fell away. Oh, yes. This was exactly what I needed.

I clambered up a protrusion shaped like a jutting rock. From there, it was only a bit of a stretch to jump onto one of the thick manmade branches. Marco followed me as I roamed higher, staying in human form himself. Maybe he thought it'd be impolite to shift when I couldn't? I was too busy exploring to care.

Here and there between the branches and ledges, objects like huge bowls were wedged, stuffed full of plush cushions. I poked at one of the pillows as I climbed past one. "Cat beds?" I said, shooting Marco an amused look.

He laughed. "Basically. We do enjoy our sleep."

He stopped on a ledge about halfway up the second story, watching me as I finished my ascent to the very top. The highest branch veered on an angle all the way to the vaulted glass roof. I scrambled up it and crouched where it bowed to take in my surroundings.

I could see over the roof of the rest of the house from here, to the tops of the pines on the other side. To the south, the suburban road was visible between the trees, stretching off into the distance. A car puttered by below me, the driver completely unaware of me perched there watching him. The view of the long drop to the ground below made my pulse thump faster.

If this was how cat shifters did things, I had to say I completely approved.

I couldn't jump through the window, but there were all sorts of possibilities for leaping my way down in here. I turned my gaze to the room beneath me. The shape and placement of the various protrusions made for their own sort of challenge. I fixed my gaze on a branch ahead of me and several feet below, bunched my muscles, and launched myself toward it.

My feet hit the artificial bark smack in the center. I grasped the sides of the branch to hold myself steady, exhilaration rushing through me. Without giving myself much time to think, I spotted an appropriate ledge and pushed off again.

The feeling of free-fall raced through me for an instant before I landed. So sharp and giddying. I glanced around and threw myself down toward one of those bowls of bedding. This time I let myself land on my hands and knees. I rolled onto my back and snuggled into the cushions.

"Okay," I said. "This *is* almost as good as the climbing part."

"And the jumping part?" Marco said, hopping onto a nearby branch. His indigo eyes glinted. "You're a pretty girl, my Princess of Flames, but you're spectacular when you come that close to flight. It lights you up."

The compliment lit me up in a totally different way. I pushed myself onto my feet. "Is this how you treat all the girls? Kidnap them and then seduce them with flattery and your awesome house?"

His eyelids lowered, his gaze turning more heated. "Not at all, princess. This is only for you."

His tone was serious enough beneath the flirting that my pulse skipped. I craved that intensity, but at the same time it sent my nerves jittering. How could I be that important to him, to anyone here, just like that?

I leapt away from those worries, up one of the other slanting branches. "Well, you haven't caught me yet," I called back to him.

I heard a laugh in his intake of breath. "Let's see if I can change that."

His feet scraped the outcroppings just beneath me. I threw myself forward faster, leaning over so I could pull myself along with my hands as well. As if I were an animal even if I still couldn't turn myself into one.

I sprang from one branch to another, dashed up that one to a ledge, and abruptly found I had no way to keep going up. I'd almost hit the roof again. Marco was halfway up the branch behind me, loping up it with perfect balance. He hadn't shifted either, but the feline in him showed in every movement.

"Ran yourself into a corner?" he teased, slowing a little to draw out his pursuit.

Oh, no. I wasn't letting him win yet. "No such thing," I informed him. Then, as he reached the edge of the platform, I flung myself off it toward a branch at least a full floor below.

The exhilaration of the fall burst through me—and tugged free a memory from long, long ago. Scrambling onto the roof of a wooden playhouse and launching myself into the air. Feeling my wings unfurl and catch the wind just for a second before my child's body hit the ground. Rolling in the grass and giggling, reveling in the glimpse of my future powers.

Mama! Mama, did you see that one?

My feet hit the branch hard. My knees jarred, and the vivid glimpse of my past slipped away. I held there, inhaling shakily, my fingers digging into the manufactured bark.

"Princess?" Marco said, lowering himself onto the branch just above me.

I shook myself, but my mind wouldn't quite settle. Where had I been in that memory? Somewhere with my mother, obviously. But not New York. That had been before New York. In a shifter community somewhere? Was that where I was supposed to go now?

I looked up at Marco. "You keep calling me 'princess.' Because my mother was pretty much queen of all the shifters."

He nodded, watching me curiously.

"She must have had some kind of official home, right?" I went on. "That people would know to come to, if they needed... I don't know, official guidance or something?"

"There are four houses that are the official property of the dragon shifter line," Marco said. "One near the center of each kin-group's main territory. She'd have moved from one to another periodically or as needs required, usually with at least one of her alpha mates. Why?"

I bit my lip. "I just wondered if maybe she might have gone back to one of those homes. When she left New York, I mean. I guess if that symbol had to do with any of them, you'd have recognized it, though, wouldn't you?"

"Most likely. And if she'd returned to prime shifter territory, she wouldn't have gone unnoticed."

So much for that lead. But that line of thinking tickled up another question. "Aaron said you all knew me back then. When I was a little kid, before Mom and I left. Were we, like, friends, or...?"

Marco's crooked smile looked softer than usual. "We saw you around, here and there. I don't think I ever spoke to you except a formal introduction after the last alpha chose me—which wasn't long before you and your mother vanished. You weren't much more than a toddler most of that time, you know."

I arched my eyebrows at him. "So you're not that much of a cradle robber?"

He laughed. "I was still a kid myself, remember. When I was ten, I was a hell of a lot more interested in climbing trees and winning races than thinking about future mates." The heat crept back into his gaze. "Of course, my interests have changed a lot since then."

"Oh, yeah?" I padded a little higher up the branch I was on, giving him a challenging glance. It was easier to turn my attention back to the present than to keep dwelling on everything I couldn't remember.

"Not convinced yet?" His grin widened. Then he sprang after me, so quickly I yelped.

Marco had obviously been holding back before. He knew this feline jungle gym a lot better than I did, after all. I clambered up the branch, jumped over another, and dashed along a ledge, but he caught up with me. Tucking his arm around me, he pulled us down into one of the bowl-like beds.

"Got you," he murmured, his face just inches from mine. He'd angled his body so it wasn't quite touching me, holding himself up by his elbow, but the warmth of him washed over me. It stirred up a wave of longing so intense I couldn't imagine fighting it.

I pushed up toward him, and he claimed my mouth with his.

The kiss radiated heat through my whole being. I looped my arm around Marco's neck, wanting him closer, harder, everywhere. He teased his teeth over my lip until I whimpered and then tipped his head to kiss me even more deeply. At my tug, his body settled against mine. My breath caught at the solid, muscular weight of him. My hips arched toward his instinctively, and he groaned.

"Yes, princess," he murmured. "That's the way."

His hand traveled up my side, sliding the silk of my blouse over my skin. He cupped my breast through my bra. His thumb swiveled over my nipple, and I gasped into his mouth. Marco smiled into the kiss, teasing that peak harder with steady, knowing strokes. My fingers traced over his cheek and tangled in his hair. The swell of pleasure inside me was rising so fast I didn't know how to rein it in, how to hold on to anything. It might just carry me away.

Marco dipped his head down to trail his lips across my jaw. His hand left my breast to slip under the hem of my shirt. His fingers eased up over my bare skin, and he nipped the tender skin of my throat. I moaned, my body trembling—and a sharp pain shot through my palm.

I stiffened, and Marco froze over me. He raised his head. The lust in his heavy-lidded eyes sent a fresh tingle through me, but the pain stopped me from getting swept up in it again.

"What's wrong?" he said.

My hand had balled into a fist. I uncurled my fingers from my palm and stared, bewildered, for a second before I understood what I was seeing.

A small blue gem shone darkly in the middle of my palm. Marco's sapphire earring. I'd nicked the stud off his ear without even realizing. And accidentally jabbed the pin into my hand. A small drop of blood was beading below it.

Marco laughed low in his throat. "My Princess of Flames and her sticky fingers." He sat back on the cushions, drawing me with him but leaving a little space between us. With his own nimble fingers, he plucked out the stud. Then he brought my hand to his mouth and slicked his tongue over the tiny wound. My heart stuttered.

But the desire coursing through me had dampened a little. I dragged in a breath. Maybe that was for the best. I still wanted him—*damn*, did I want him—but at least I felt in control again.

Marco tucked the earring into his pocket. He kept my hand in his, but he didn't pull me to him again. Could he sense my hesitation?

"This thieving habit of yours is a bit of a strange one," he remarked, with an easy smile. "Should I be worried you'll end up robbing me out of house and home before the end of the day?"

He spoke so lightly I couldn't help smiling back. "I, um, might also have pocketed a mirror from the guest bedroom. That's it so far. I'm sorry. It's kind of a nervous habit."

Marco cocked his head. "Can I ask how exactly one develops stealing as a habit?"

My chest tightened, but he was looking at me with so little judgment that a moment later I started to relax. The four guys here were sharing so much of themselves with me. Maybe it was only fair they had a better idea who they were letting into their lives.

"When I first lost my apartment, I didn't have anywhere to go," I said. The words stuck in my throat, but I pushed them out. "Mom had always warned me about the police and any kind of government authority, so they didn't seem safe. I ended up getting in with a group of street kids this guy named Fisher had sort of... hired on. He owned a building where he'd let us sleep as long as we'd bring him stuff we'd stolen every day. And he'd give us a small cut of what he got fencing the stuff, so we could buy food and all that. I didn't *like* doing it, because I know it's wrong, but I was good at it, because of how fast I can be. And I didn't know what else to do."

Marco stroked his fingertips over the back of my head soothingly. "I think we've all been in positions where we had to do things we'd rather not for our own survival. There's no shame in that, princess."

There was, though. The shame of it still burned my cheeks when I thought about it. "I didn't get away from Fisher until I was almost twenty. Kylie helped me. But it took a long time even after I met her, because he didn't want me to go. I was his best thief. I was scared of what he'd do... But I did get away, in the end, and I haven't *meant* to steal anything in more than a year."

I'd been looking at my hands through my entire confession. Finally I lifted my gaze to Marco's face. His eyes were gentle, but his tone was as dry and cocky as ever.

"So my princess is a tough girl. I can't say I have any complaints there."

The last of the tension inside me released. I gave his shoulder a playful shove. "It seems like you're a tough guy yourself. What's the story with that scar?"

I motioned to his eyebrow. The second the question came out, I knew I shouldn't have asked it. Marco's muscles tensed where his body was still aligned with mine. Shit. I opened my mouth to say never mind, and just then my butt vibrated.

Or rather, my phone vibrated against my butt. I

squirmed a little farther away from Marco into the cushions and tugged it out. In the first instant I read the alert on the screen, every other concern faded from my mind.

"Kylie texted me," I said, springing to my feet. "She found someone who recognized the symbol from my locket."

CHAPTER 11

Ren

"It's right in the middle of vampire territory," Nate said, crossing his arms over his brawny chest where he stood by the arm of the sofa. "We can't just saunter on in there and expect them to give us a free pass."

"My scouts move through the city on a regular basis without any trouble whatsoever," Marco replied. He leaned back in the sitting room's armchair. "As long as we don't draw attention to ourselves, they'll never even realize we were there. I know stealth isn't your strong point, but you can manage not to lumber about like a total bear, can't you?"

Nate scowled at him. West paused where he'd been pacing back and forth near the door. "How do we know this information is even worth following up on? We're hearing it third hand."

My fingers tightened around my phone. I sat up

straighter where I'd curled up at one end of the sofa. "Kylie knows the people she talks to. If she didn't think this guy was legit, she wouldn't have told me about it." She'd reported that a guy she played pool with sometimes did urban "explorations." He'd been pretty sure he'd seen the inverted flame image in a tunnel leading to one of New York City's abandoned subway stations.

"Why would anything to do with shifters be down in some abandoned subway tunnel?" Nate asked.

By the fireplace, Aaron raised his head. "The spot could have been chosen for exactly that reason, if the dragon shifters wanted to keep it hidden. No ordinary shifter would stumble across it there. But Nate is right. It'll be difficult for all four of us to enter the city together without any of the locals noticing. Which is why—"

"All *five* of us," I broke in.

He blinked at me, his clear blue eyes momentarily puzzled. "What?"

I gestured to the bunch of us. "You said 'all four of us.' But we're five. I'm coming too, obviously."

Apparently that fact wasn't so obvious. Aaron's mouth tensed, and Nate bristled as if his bear really were coming out.

"No," the bigger guy said. "It's dangerous enough with just us. Our job is to make sure you're protected, and that means you stay here."

"I was going to suggest that only one, or at most two, of the alphas should investigate," Aaron said in his light, even voice. "There's no need for even all four of us to go."

"Well, even if only one or two of you goes, I'm coming with." I waved my phone in the air. "I'm the one who got the information, remember? I'm the one it's *for*. The symbol was in my locket. It's some kind of message from my mother. If *anyone* goes, it should be me."

Nate shook his head. "If it wasn't vampire territory, I'd never argue with you. But you don't understand the full situation. It's not worth the risk, especially when the tip might not be reliable."

Marco's gaze darted between us, his expression somewhere between contemplative and amused. He wasn't telling me to stay home, but he wasn't leaping to support me either. The one voice in my favor was West's, although of course he had to say it in the most insulting way possible.

"If she's going to be head of all shifter-kin, she'd better be able to hold her own," he growled. "Let her come. It'll give her a taste of the supernatural world outside this ridiculous house."

Marco raised an eyebrow at that. "If you don't enjoy the comforts in here, you're welcome to sleep in the yard tonight."

"Who cares about the house?" I said. "If I *am* going to be head of all the shifters, I should get to make a few decisions for myself. And I say I'm going. You have no idea what we might be looking for. For all we know, my mom set it up so I'm the only one who can find it or figure out what to do with it. Won't making *one* trip *with* me draw a lot less attention than two trips when you realize you need me there after all?"

"You could stay nearby, ready to join us if we let you know your presence was needed," Aaron suggested.

"No. No way. I haven't had a say in *any* of this so far,

but this could be my mother's last message to me. I have to see it for myself."

"Ren," Nate started, but West broke in.

"You're all too hung up on the past. This is a totally different scenario. Vampires had nothing to do with what happened before."

"If we *do* piss them off, vampires are plenty dangerous," Marco said. "We shouldn't completely dismiss them."

"Hold on," I said, setting down my phone. My fingers curled around the arm of the sofa. "What 'past scenario' are you talking about? Why *are* you so worried about protecting me? What—"

A splinter of a memory jabbed through my mind. Just a fragment, wavering and incomplete, but with a jolt of panic that brought a metallic flavor into my mouth.

I was huddled on the floor, clutching the arm of a girl a little older than me, pale with a head of blond ringlets. Her mouth was set in a thin, bloodless line. Another girl, even older, stood at my other side, black waves cascading down her trembling back. Her hand was braced against my head, too tense to really comfort.

The three of us were staring at my mother—my mother and the rugged, barrel-chested man who was arguing with her. I knew that low, hoarse voice had usually wrapped me up in comfort, but now it only made my pulse skitter.

"You have to go. Now."

"I have to stay and fight for what's mine," my mother insisted, her eyes flashing.

An agonized cry rang out. My mother flinched, and

the man's expression shuttered. "There are too many of them. If you try to fight here, you'll lose your chance to fight your way out. Go. For them."

He swept his arm toward us—and the memory flicked away.

I slumped forward on the sofa, dropping my head into my hands. The immediacy of the moment was gone, but my sense of it was still trickling in. That man—he'd been one of my fathers. *Daddy*, some part of me called out with a pang. And the girls beside me...

I looked up, bracing my hands on either side of my neck. The guys had all fallen silent, watching me. My mouth was dry. I swallowed hard.

"I had sisters," I said in a ragged voice. "Two of them, older than me. Didn't I? Why did my mother run away with me and not them? What *happened* to them? What happened to my fathers?"

Nate and Aaron exchanged a glance. Marco opened his mouth and hesitated. West looked as if he'd swallowed his tongue, the one time I actually wanted him to let it loose.

"Tell me," I snapped. "Why do you keep trying to hide it? What are you all so afraid will happen to me?"

"Ren," Nate said roughly. He sank onto the sofa beside me. "It's not that we wanted to hide it from you. We just wanted to give you a chance to adjust before you had to deal with that too."

"With what?" I said, my voice suddenly small. It was horrible, whatever it was. I didn't need him to tell me that. The memory and their reactions stunk of it.

Aaron drew in a breath. "A band of rogue shifters

attacked your family one night, sixteen years ago," he said quietly. "As far as anyone knows, their goal was to kill you, your mother, and your sisters—all of the dragon shifters—and the four alphas, who were there with you that night. Your fathers died trying to stop them from getting to you. The rogues caught your sisters and murdered them too. Your mother barely made it out alive with you."

I'd been braced for his explanation, but the words rocked me anyway. My stomach churned. Nate offered his arm, and I scooted closer to him, letting him pull me into an embrace. The reassurance of his strong body barely took the edge off my horror.

"And then she ran," I filled in. "All the way to New York City. She was afraid they'd try again." That was why she'd tried to keep us so invisible. Why she'd been so scared she'd felt she had to block my memories and my powers.

"From what you've told us, we have to assume that's the case," Aaron said.

"And I for one can't blame her," Marco put in. "She kept you safe—and hopefully herself too. She did what she had to do." He shot West a sharp look as if daring him to argue, but the wolf shifter had withdrawn to the doorway, his face shadowed.

"But *why*?" I burst out. "Why would anyone want to hurt us like that?" The remembered cry rang in my ears—the horrible pain in it. The image of my sisters' faces... Neither of them could have been older than ten. And these rogues had just *slaughtered* them?

"No one knows for sure," Nate said, rubbing my arm.

"Your fathers and your mother killed a bunch of the rogues defending themselves, but of course the dead can't say anything. The ones who survived got out of there before anyone else realized what was going on. They were never caught."

"Most likely it was a power grab," Aaron said. "Most of the shifters who refuse to ally themselves with their kin-group are carrying a lot of bitterness and anger. They don't like the way the rules are made or who carries them out. Maybe they thought they could set themselves up as the new alphas. Maybe they just wanted to sow disorder. If we're lucky, we'll never encounter them again, so we'll never need to know."

"But if that group is still out there, and there's no reason to think they aren't, the first thing they'll want to do if they find out you're alive is finish the job they started," Marco said in a darker tone than usual. He lifted his chin toward Nate. "Which is why bear boy has gone into overprotective mode."

"I don't think there's anything *over* about it," Nate muttered. "Do you see why I'd rather you stayed here, Ren? No one except us and Marco's few people here know we've even found you yet. The longer we can keep it that way, the more time we can buy before we might have to deal with the rogues again."

Right. More time for me to come into the powers that seemed stubbornly locked inside me, so I'd have any hope at all of defending myself.

A shiver ran through me. There were people out there who hated me so much they'd wanted to kill me when I'd been a helpless five-year-old.

And if they succeeded this time, what would happen to the shifters then? If I was the last dragon, and I died without passing on that line... My kind would be extinct. There'd be nothing left tying the kin-groups together.

My sense of shifter society was still vague, but that thought chilled me to the core. I wrapped my hand around Nate's. I did understand why he was so worried, why Aaron had argued in favor of caution too, why Marco hadn't spoken up for me. They needed me... and the alphas before them had already failed once.

I needed them too. I felt a connection to all four of the men around me, humming through the air. Even as the chill prickled through me, that connection steadied me.

I wasn't alone anymore. I had them now, like I was meant to. I couldn't keep running.

Mom had taken my memories, but not forever. I knew what I was now, and I needed to keep remembering.

I was a dragon.

I pushed myself away from Nate, with a squeeze of his hand to tell him it wasn't a rejection. "I get it," I said, standing up. "I don't blame you for worrying. But I'm still coming. It's the path my mother left for me to follow, and I'm not letting anyone stop me."

CHAPTER 12

Nate

OUR DRAGON SHIFTER was so strong. She sat squeezed between me and Marco in the back of Aaron's sedan as he drove the bunch of us into the city, her back straight and her jaw set. But I'd taken her hand a few minutes after we'd gotten in, and she hadn't let go of mine since. Her slim fingers stayed twined with mine, gripping tight.

They felt so fragile, but I knew the rest of her wasn't. The news about her family's murders had shocked her— that was obvious. I was never going to forget the way the blood had drained from her face as Aaron had told her the story, as if she were dying alongside her long-gone sisters and fathers. But she hadn't let her emotions hold her back. She wasn't letting anything stop her from being right here with us to face whatever waited ahead.

I had to admit, I *hated* that Ren was here. My hackles

had risen the second we'd crossed the city's boundaries. I hadn't scented a vampire yet, but the whole place stunk of metal and burnt gasoline. Even if there hadn't been any bloodsuckers around, this wasn't where shifters were meant to go. I had to admire Ren too, though. She might not have remembered much yet, but she was still every inch a dragon.

As soon as we'd figured out what had happened to her mother, we could get on with our proper lives. The way we'd all been waiting to for the last sixteen years. Alphas and dragon shifter, all the kin-groups growing in harmony.

As long as the other alphas didn't screw it up. West sat in the front passenger seat with that perpetual cloud over him, his expression grim. "Isn't there a way to avoid all this traffic?" he muttered to Aaron as we crept down a jammed street. He'd been so cold to Ren the entire time. How could he really think that pushing her aside, throwing away the legacy of the dragon shifters, was the right move?

And Marco... You could never really trust a cat. He lounged on the other side of the backseat with his elbow propped against the window. "Heel, doggie," he teased. "We'll get there when we get there." Which only made West's frown turn into a scowl. The feline alpha had welcomed Ren, sure, but he also took a little too much enjoyment from stirring up trouble.

"I can turn onto a street that should be less congested up here," Aaron said calmly. The avian alpha seemed steady enough, but the avians didn't mingle much with the rest of us anyway. I wasn't sure how to read him.

The bear-kin and those we ruled over had never wavered in our devotion to shifter law. *I* would stand by Ren no matter what happened. At least she could be sure of that.

I ran my thumb over the back of her hand, and she leaned a little more of her weight on me. I resisted the urge to nuzzle her hair and take in her lovely scent. For now I had to stay focused on protecting her. All the other pleasures of having a mate could wait until our business here was finished.

But I was looking forward to them even more now that I'd met her.

Aaron drew the car to a stop. "From here, we need to go on foot," he said. Ren looked up at me with a smile that sent a bolt of desire through my chest. Resolve coiled around it.

She was leaving this city alive, or I'd die here too.

Ren

I braced my hand against the wall of the tunnel, and my fingers came away damp and gritty. My nose wrinkled at the sensation. The stairs we were tramping down were narrow, the air dank, and the space dark except for the bobbing beam of Aaron's flashlight as he led the way.

I'd never been really claustrophobic, but this place gave me the creeps. Nowhere to run or jump.

Nowhere to stretch the wings I couldn't convince to rise out of me yet.

At least I had my best friend with me again. Kylie squeezed my other hand where she was walking shoulder-to-shoulder with me and shot me a grin. *She* seemed more excited about this expedition than I was. Maybe because she hadn't just heard a story about practically her entire family being slaughtered.

"Do you have any idea what we're going to find down here?" she murmured. "I mean, why your mom wanted to send you to that symbol?"

I shook my head. "I don't know any more than you do at this point." About my mom's plans, at least. The second we'd met up by the subway entrance, Kylie had asked how I was, but I hadn't mentioned what I'd learned about my past. It seemed like a lot to dump on even my best friend. I was still processing the facts myself.

I must have seen more of the violence than the brief fragment of memory that had come to me, but none of the rest had come back yet, even after hearing the story. I wasn't sure if that was for the best or if I'd rather have had those images to examine. I could almost sense them, like sharks weaving by beneath water too dark to penetrate in my mind. They were going to surface sometime, and when they did, it was going to hurt.

"Quite an adventure," Kylie said, and nudged me with her elbow. "You looked like you were getting pretty close with the big guy. Now he's a hunk and a half."

She must have meant Nate. He was at the back of our procession, several feet behind us, making sure no unfriendly intruders snuck up on us. My face warmed a little. I was getting used to the idea that all four of these guys were meant to be my partners, but I knew it was going to sound kind of weird to anyone else. Anyone human, at least.

But it wasn't as if I'd be able to hide it from Kylie very long. I didn't want to.

"Actually..." I said. "I've been getting pretty close with all of them. Well, the three of them who don't spend the whole time glaring daggers at me." I glowered briefly at West's lean back where he was stalking along just behind Aaron. "It turns out that's the thing with dragon shifters. We're supposed to, er, bond with all of the alphas. It's, like, a political decree."

We followed the guys past a door with squeaky hinges and into a wider tunnel that was just as dark and dank. Aaron's light wavered over the curved walls of the long-unused subway route.

Kylie's eyebrows had shot up. "Wait. When you say *bond*, you mean in a fully bodily way, right?"

The flush in my cheeks deepened. "That's the idea. We haven't gotten *that* far yet."

I braced myself for shock or disgust, but Kylie just laughed. She held up her hand for a high five. "You go, girl. If I had a chance to handle four guys like this at the same time, you'd better believe I'd go for it. What a way to give up your V-card!"

In that moment, I wished I hadn't admitted to her that I'd never gone all the way with a guy. "I'm pretty sure it won't be all of them at the same time," I said. So far they'd only reached out to me one at a time. The thought of more than one of them kissing me, touching me, together sent a sudden warmth through my body.

Maybe I didn't entirely hate the idea. But this wasn't really the time to be exploring *that*.

Kylie's expression turned a shade more serious. "You *are* okay, aren't you? Are you sure you can trust everything they've been telling you?"

"Yeah. I remember enough that it all makes sense. It's overwhelming, but at the same time, I feel more like myself the more I find out." I paused. "*You* don't think it's totally crazy, do you? I mean, shifters and vampires and who the hell knows what else?"

"Please. Of course it's crazy. But that doesn't mean I can't believe it. I saw Hunk-and-a-Half turn into a bear with my very own eyes. And I know you've got a good head on your shoulders. That's why I need you around."

She looped her arm around me to give me a quick sideways hug. The gesture sent a pang through my chest. How much longer *would* I be around? When—if—I did manage to take on the full role of dragon shifter, I couldn't hang out in Brooklyn with Kylie all the time.

We could figure that out later. After we'd figured out whatever it was Mom had wanted me to understand.

Aaron's voice rang out. "It's here." He was pointing the flashlight at a spot on one of the walls. The rest of us picked our way closer over the cracked cement and abandoned tracks. The air shifted, sending a cool chill over my arms. I rubbed at the goose bumps.

The wall had been built out of interlocking stones. The circle of light illuminated a rectangular one that had been carved with a symbol like the one in my locket: an upside-down flame in the midst of a spiral. My heartbeat kicked up a notch.

"That's really it," I said.

I glanced around, as if Mom might step out of the shadows now that I was here. As if she could have been waiting down here all this time, or even just since my birthday.

No one stirred in the darkness except West's tense form. Then Marco and Nate prowled closer to the stone. Nate prodded it first before stepping back.

Marco tested its edges with his more lithe fingers. "It doesn't seem all that eager to offer up its secrets," he remarked.

"They're not secrets meant for you," I said. This was why I'd insisted on coming. I walked up to the wall, into the glow of the flashlight. Up close, the symbol sent a tingle through my body. It drew my hands to it. I raised my arms and pressed my palms to either side of the flame, the way it seemed to want.

The stone jolted toward me with a scraping sound, and my mind cracked apart. The sensations of the tunnel washed away in a wave of memories.

I was a little girl, dashing through the forest to find a hiding spot before one of my daddies finished counting. The lush green smells of late spring surrounded me. I ducked behind a tree and swallowed a giggle.

Me and my sisters danced around our mother in time with the pop song she'd started playing on her old boombox. She grasped each of our hands in turn, spinning us around. Our feet pattered over the wooden floor.

We sat in a row along the edge of a platform where Mama was holding audience. The edge was high enough and my legs short enough that I could swing my feet without touching the floor. The shifters approached our mother one by one. We whispered to each other, guessing each shifter's animal by scent and mannerisms. "That one's got to be a badger." "No, no, I'd say raccoon."

We were running down the hall, Mama urging us faster. My pulse thundered in my ears. We had to get outside, outside where Mama could shift and fight. An immense lioness sprang from a doorway, snapping her jaws around my sister's arm with a burst of bright red blood. A shriek broke from my throat.

And on and on. The fractured memories hit me as if from inside and out at the same time, bubbling up through my head and pouring into me from the stone. I was drowning in them.

Then they stuttered to a halt. My mind went blank. My mother's voice washed over me, soft and lilting.

I'm so sorry it had to be this way, Serenity. I did the best I could to keep you safe. Follow the crystal—

There was a sound like an intake of breath. It jerked me back to reality.

I was standing in front of the subway tunnel wall. My fingers clutched the cool stone slab the flame symbol was carved into. It had popped out of the wall, revealing a dark hollow. The alphas and Kylie still stood around me, waiting.

My legs wobbled. Aaron leapt to my side to place a steadying hand on my shoulder. I leaned into him, trying to make sense of my swirling thoughts.

"I remember," I said. But that wasn't totally true. My

head felt stuffed full of the early childhood I'd just recovered, but the memories jostled against each other with ragged edges. They didn't entirely feel like mine yet. There were still gaps and fuzzy bits. Whatever Mom had done to suppress them, it hadn't been an exact magic.

"What's in there?" Kylie asked.

I focused my gaze on the hollow. Something pale and flat lay on the rough surface inside. I set the stone down and tugged the hidden object out, my fingertips sliding over a polished surface.

It was a clear circle, like glass but with a brighter sparkle, twice the width of my palm. A faint pattern of lines and dots was etched into its surface. I squinted at it, trying to make sense of them, but they didn't form letters or even definite shapes.

Follow the crystal, my mother's voice had said. I guessed this was the crystal. How the hell was I supposed to *follow* it?

I swiveled, turning it in my hands as if that might trigger some kind of pull, and a tapping sounded farther down the tunnel. My body froze. The guys whipped around to peer in the same direction.

Several figures approached us, materializing out of the shadows. They stopped at the edge of Aaron's light. Nine men and women, all slim with deep-set eyes. Their skin ranged from pale to darker brown, but all of them had a slightly sallow look to them, as if they'd been too long out of the sun.

Oh. Understanding prickled over me at the same time as their papery acidic smell reached my nose. I'd never met one of their kind before, but I knew exactly what I was looking at all the same.

It wasn't vampires who'd threatened my family before, but it sure as hell was now.

CHAPTER 13

Ren

ONE OF THE vampires opened his narrow mouth, tasting the air with a snake-like swipe of his tongue. Thin fangs glinted behind his lips. I repressed a shudder.

"Shifters," he said, wrinkling his nose in distaste. "You're far from home, aren't you? This is our territory. There are penalties for infringing on it, as you should well know."

Smarmy bastards, weren't they? I stepped back, closer to the wall, but my hackles had risen. If they were threatening my alphas, they were going to have to contend with me as well.

"We didn't think there was any harm in taking a little stroll," Marco tossed out. "Checking out the sights, enjoying a change in scenery."

A couple of the vampires glanced around as if seriously wondering whether shifters thought subway tunnels were scenic. The one who'd spoken to us sneered.

"We don't have time for games."

Marco shrugged. "Funny, I'd have thought being immortal meant you had all the time in the world."

"What are you doing here?" the vampire demanded. "You wouldn't have come this far into our domain without reason."

"That might be true." West said, folding his arms over his chest. It was nice to see his glower directed at people who deserved it for once—if you could call vampires "people." "But you can forget it if you think we're going to stand around and chat with you. Back off, and we'll go."

The vampires did the exact opposite of backing off. They slunk closer, more fangs gleaming in the crowd now. Nate edged closer to me, his muscles tensed, looking ready to jump in front of me if need be.

"Answer my questions, or we'll simply destroy you," the vampire said. "Then your purpose won't matter one way or another."

Aaron stepped forward, his hands raised. "We apologize for this intrusion into your territory," he said. "And I apologize for my friends' rudeness. We had an urgent matter that didn't leave us time to parlay with your leaders. I swear by the moon and earth we came with no ill intentions, and we would leave just as peacefully."

"It's too late for that," a woman near the back of the vampire pack hissed. "You came uninvited. You must pay the consequences for that."

"Holy shit," Kylie said to me out of the corner of her mouth. "This is a little freakier than I was prepared for."

Me too. I grabbed her hand, tugging her closer to me. I wasn't letting *her* get hurt, especially when she'd only come down here to help me. We should have just gotten the instructions from her and gone down on our own. But I'd selfishly wanted the chance to talk to her—the one person from my old life I *could* still talk to.

"Please," Aaron was saying. "There's no need for this to come to violence. We've finished our business here. It was a shifter matter, nothing to do with your kind. If you—"

"Enough talk," the first vampire snapped. His cold gaze settled on me. "Something about this one smells strange. Not like any beast I recognize." His eyes narrowed. "What *are* you?"

He snapped his fingers, and the vampire beside him darted toward me as if to haul me over. Nate pushed between us with a growl. He shoved the vampire back toward the group, so hard the young man fell on his ass.

"Don't you dare touch her."

The lead vampire grimaced. "This is our domain. We take what we want. If you refuse to obey, you will not remain."

Just like that, the vampires sprang at us in a single flickering motion. A yelp broke from my throat. I yanked Kylie back as the four alphas threw themselves forward to meet the vampire's charge.

They shifted as they ran. Nate's form bulged through his clothing, looming into the grizzly bear I'd met in Marco's sitting room yesterday. Only he was no teddy bear now. He lunged forward, smacking one vampire's head against the wall with a sickening thud, swiping his massive paw at another that tried to dodge past him.

A golden eagle swooped from a heap of clothes and dove with claws extended to catch one of the vampires in the face. Aaron's battle cry rang through the tunnel. The beam of the fallen flashlight sparked across the bright feathers of his huge wings.

A wolf kicked out of West's jeans, his ruddy silver-tipped fur gleaming in the wavering light. He clamped his jaws around one of the vampire's legs and heaved. The vampire tumbled to the tunnel floor with a crack of her head against one of the subway rails. The wolf whirled to charge at another attacker. Something gleamed starker red on his chest. Had she hurt him?

A large black jaguar pounced into the fray. Marco knocked another vampire onto the ground, pinning him. His sleek tail lashed back and forth as he slapped the vampire across the cheek. The crack of a broken neck echoed off the walls.

The violence was horrifying, but at the same time the strength and speed of my shifter mates took my breath away. These weren't just forms they put on like some kind of costume. They *were* those animals, down to the center of their being, and they moved like magic.

My hand squeezed tighter around Kylie's. My heart was thumping in the base of my throat. The guys had taken down some of the vampires, but the others were still fighting, swinging daggers and baring their fangs. I should be out there with my mates, doing my part. It was for me that all of us were down here.

But what could I do with this human body against those undead creatures? In the damp tunnel air, I suddenly felt more useless than I ever had in my life. I had no weapons, no claws except the ones scrabbling in my chest. If I threw myself in there and tried to fight, all I'd be doing was giving the vampires a chance to grab me and turn the tables on the alphas.

If I could shift... If I could join them as an equal, prove I was worthy of the risks they were taking for me...

I pushed Kylie toward the wall. "Stay there," I said. "No matter what. Don't get any closer to them."

She nodded, at a rare loss for words. I balled my hands, staring into the midst of the fight. I knew how the transformation was supposed to feel. I'd glimpsed the feeling in my memories. That stretching, unfurling sensation that would rip through my body. I wanted it now, so badly.

I reached inside to the frantic scraping of those internal claws. *Burst out. Break free. Let loose the dragon inside.* I *was* that dragon. I knew it, as much as I'd known my mother when I'd seen her scaled form flying overhead in my memory. I could taste the charring of fiery breath on my tongue.

But my body didn't comply. My form stayed completely human. The dragon remained locked inside me. I groaned, wrenching at myself with all my will, and it was still me just standing there.

My memories had been unlocked. Mom's magic had fallen away. Why was it still so hard for me to follow my true nature?

In front of me, a vampire slashed at Nate's side,

drawing a dark red streak through his bear's chestnut fur. He bellowed and swung his paw, but his attacker darted away. Another bloodsucker was struggling on the ground with Marco. She sank her fangs deep into the jaguar's foreleg, and he let out a pained snarl.

The memory of the lioness sinking her teeth into my sister flashed through my mind. It shook loose other fragments, bits of the past I didn't want in my head right now. A warthog stabbing its tusks into the side of a great tawny mountain lion. *Daddy*. A polished floor streaked with blood. My mother's fingers clutching mine so tight a stabbing pain shot through my bones. A whimper fading into a gurgle with the slitting of a throat.

A hoarse rumbling chuckle that seemed to echo all around me, rising higher as the blood flowed faster.

My stomach flipped, threatening to spew my hasty lunch up my throat. I gripped the wall to keep my balance.

"Ren!" Kylie said. She hugged me from behind. I let myself sag into her just for a second, and then I pushed myself forward.

I had to help somehow. I couldn't stand back through another massacre.

I flailed for some kind of weapon. A length of bent pipe lay by the opposite wall. I snatched it up, spun around to look for a target to whack across the head—and stopped.

There was no one left to whack. While I'd been caught up in my memories, my alphas had finished the job. The wolf was just backing away from a vampire whose throat he'd gouged out. The grizzly slammed our last conscious attacker against the wall one more time, and the bloodsucker slumped onto the ground. Aaron and Marco had already shifted back into human form. Blood dappled Marco's arm and side, and Aaron limped a bit as he moved toward his discarded clothes, but otherwise they looked fine.

And I mean *fine*. Even with fighting adrenaline still rushing through my veins, I couldn't help appreciating the full view of their impressive physiques. The gods had really outdone themselves when they made this quartet of men.

Aaron's impressive, er, apparatus and equally spectacular ass disappeared into his boxers and then his jeans. Marco sauntered over to another of the fallen vampires, looking as if he didn't mind showing off all his equipment to anyone who felt like taking an eyeful. No, he definitely didn't mind at all. He shot me a glance over his well-muscled shoulder and winked at me. My face flushed.

"Ren," Nate said, man again. He strode toward me and then stopped as if realizing his big, brawny body plus nakedness might be a little overwhelming. I suspected his clothes hadn't survived his transformation. Aaron shoved his shirt into Nate's hands. Nate gave me a sheepish smile as he tied it around his waist for makeshift modesty. "Are you all right? They didn't get to you?"

I shook my head and looked over at Kylie. She was okay too, but her knuckles were white where she'd balled her hands around the hem of her tank top. "Is it over?" I asked. "Did you... kill all of them?"

"They're not dead," Marco said, nudging one guy's

leg with his toe. "Or, not any more dead than they already were. But they won't be bothering us anytime soon."

"When vampires are injured severely enough, they go into stasis while they heal," Aaron explained. "They'll be out for a few hours at least."

"They didn't bargain for running into a bunch of alphas," Marco said flippantly. "That'll teach them to be that cocky."

Aaron shot him a warning look. "We don't want to be cocky either. They may have backup on the way. They'll definitely be reporting the clash as soon as they've recovered. When they do, the local vampire lord isn't going to be happy with us. They *did* have the right to question and attack us after finding us on their territory."

Marco shrugged, but Nate's expression had darkened. "We need to get Ren out of here fast, then."

Aaron nodded. "I don't think it's a good idea to stay at Marco's house any longer either. That's the first place they'll come looking for shifters who've recently passed through. Are there any shifter settlements we can make it to today while still giving ourselves some distance?"

West sighed. My gaze jerked to him. I hadn't noticed him shifting back, and now he'd already gotten his clothes back on. He was just buttoning up his shirt, a patch of white that looked like a bandage disappearing under the fabric, along with a six pack that would have made most pro athletes cry with envy. Even if he was a jerk, I found I was a little disappointed to have missed the full view.

Then he started talking again. Unfortunately.

"My kin has a village just south of Morgantown,

West Virginia," he said in a clearly reluctant tone. "Or do you want to cower even farther away than that?"

Aaron gave him a measured look. "I think that'll do." He turned to Kylie. "You don't have to come with us if you'd rather stay here, but I think you'd be better off spending a little while out of town. If the vampires caught your scent, you could become a target."

Kylie openly ogled his bare—and buff—chest and gave him a sly grin. "Oh, don't worry, I'd *much* rather hang out with you guys than those creeps." She held out her hand to me. "Road trip! Just like we always wanted."

I managed to smile as I twined my fingers with hers. This wasn't the road trip I'd been imagining I'd take with my bestie. For one, I'd have preferred to kick it off with fewer semi-dead bodies. And to go without the threat of vampire vengeance hanging over us along the way.

CHAPTER 14

Ren

FOR THE THIRD time in as many days, I woke up in an unfamiliar bed. With no air conditioning in this home that was more cabin than house, the heat of the late June morning hung thick in the air. I'd kicked off my blanket, and the sheet was twisted around my legs.

I sat up on the twin bed, taking in the room I'd only seen in semi-darkness when we'd arrived late last night. A few of West's canine shifter kin-folk had put us up for the time being.

Kylie was sprawled on the matching bed across from me, her face buried in the pillow. A faint snore drifted up from it. The only other furniture in the room was a well-worn rug, a cedar wardrobe that gave off a sweetly pungent scent, and a stool by the window. Daylight streamed in across the wooden floor.

I peeled off my sheet and poked around in the bag

I'd packed before our rushed departure from the city. The guys had given Kylie and me the okay to stop by our apartment briefly, so I had a few sets of my own clothes, not Marco's fancy get-up. Since it seemed possible we might need to run—or fight—again, I grabbed a pair of sweats and a comfortable tee. Once I was dressed, I pulled the dark waves of my hair back into a braid.

Mom used to braid my hair, when I was little. The ghost of her fingers brushed over the nape of my neck as I twisted and wove. My throat tightened.

Follow the crystal, her voice had told me yesterday. I'd spent an awful lot of the drive to West Virginia staring at that crystal slab, and I still had no idea how I was supposed to follow it anywhere. If the pattern on it was supposed to tell me, I was still at a loss. It just looked like a random jumble of lines and dots to me.

Why did you have to go, Mom? I thought at her, wherever the hell she was. *Why couldn't you have stayed so we could do this together? Why didn't you explain anything before you left?*

I couldn't get any answer to those questions right now, of course. I sighed and eased open the door.

The house was either empty or other inhabitants were still sleeping. The spread on the kitchen table suggested *someone* had already come through. A rich sugary smell wafted off fresh-baked blueberry scones. I hesitated, but the table was obviously set in anticipation of guests. I grabbed one, slathered some butter on it, and walked toward the front door as I took a bite.

The crumbly pastry melted on my tongue. That was

heaven, right there. I closed my eyes, savoring it. Then I peeked outside.

The village we'd stopped in was apparently entirely made up of shifters. Aaron had told me more about shifter culture during the drive down. From what he'd said, it was pretty common for shifters to set up communities of their own, keeping the illusion of being normal human beings to anyone who happened to pass by, but having a little more freedom to be themselves the rest of the time. "It's easier than constantly being on the alert, remembering you have to blend in."

Standing on the cabin's doorstep, looking across the packed earth of what appeared to be the village common, I could see the appeal. Most of the people ambling into the shops or chatting with friends looked like regular human beings. But over here a group of older teens were preening, a few of them experimenting with letting their canine ears protrude from their human hair. Over there, a couple of foxes who must have gone out for a morning run ducked into their house through a swinging back door. There was a sense of openness in the air that made it hard for yesterday's worries to follow me.

As I watched, a familiar figure came into view at the edge of the common. The morning sunlight caught on the silver mixed into West's light auburn hair, reminding me of the silver-tipped ruddy fur of his wolf form. He was walking beside an elderly woman who was gesturing as she talked. When she finished, he said something to her that made her face light up.

West took her hands in his and bowed his head to

her. As he let go, she patted him affectionately on the cheek. Then she shuffled away, smiling.

A couple of the teens sauntered over. From their expressions, whatever they said was pretty cheeky. West gave the first boy a playful cuff to the ears. They feinted back and forth a bit, West clearly giving the boy space to try his strength. He let the younger guy get in a few taps of his fists before grabbing him in a quick flip and setting him down on his ass.

The boy shook his head with a rueful laugh, and West grinned—a real, relaxed grin, not the tense smiles that were the most I'd seen from him before now. An ache filled my chest as the bond between us tugged at me. That man over there, acting the alpha for his people... That was a man I could really fall for.

As if he'd sensed my gaze, West looked my way. Our eyes locked. A flicker of heat passed through me, speeding up my pulse.

I shouldn't just stand here and gawk, right? I pushed myself off the cabin's front step and ambled into the common.

The two teens standing with West peered at me as I approached. At first I thought it was just normal curiosity. But one of them waved to the rest of their group. Before I'd even reached West, I found myself surrounded. They looked me over from head to toe with subtle twitches of their noses.

"You're the dragon shifter," one of them said in an awed tone. "This is so cool! We're, like, the first people to meet you now that you're back."

"Oh," I said, feeling awkward. "Yeah, I guess so. It's good to meet you too?"

"I *have* to see you shift," one of the guys said. "It must be amazing."

"Er..."

"Kids!" a woman's voice rang out. A middle-aged couple had come up on our group. The woman shooed the teens back. She turned to me. "I'm so sorry. They don't know the proper respect, at their age, and it being so long... It's an honor to offer our hospitality to you."

"History in the making," her husband agreed. He squeezed my hand briefly with a pleased smile.

More people were emerging from their houses and the shops around us. My chest started to constrict. My fingers itched. I jerked them back toward my body—too late. A warm metal circle pressed against my palm. I'd snagged the woman's ring without even meaning to.

An embarrassed heat flooded my face. I ducked down and pretended to pick it up off the ground. "I think you dropped this," I said, handing the ring to her.

"Oh! Thank you so much. I can't think of how that slipped off."

I bit my tongue. A larger crowd was congregating around me. Murmurs of "Dragon shifter!" passed from person to person. "I talked to her first!" one of the teen girls was bragging.

What did they expect me to do? I sure as hell hoped they weren't waiting for me to demonstrate my awesome —and completely non-existent—shifting powers.

West wove through the gathering crowd. For the first time since I'd met him, I had to say I was glad to see him.

He gave me a terse smile, but his dark green eyes were softer than usual.

"I think we have a few things to discuss between the two of us," he said, loud enough for the villagers to hear. They hung back while he ushered me back toward the house where I'd spent the night. His hand brushed the back of my bare arm. Even as overwhelmed as I was, my awareness of his body, just inches from mine, tingled into sharper focus.

West stopped when we were out of hearing distance and stepped to the side to give me more space. I felt that separation, too, like a tearing inside me. Whatever I thought about the wolf alpha and his attitude, some part of me wanted him next to me very, very badly.

"They, um, really are enthusiastic," I said, hoping my longing wasn't obvious.

West rubbed his jaw, which was covered with a light shading of stubble that made his handsome face even more appealing. He looked back toward the village common. "They've been waiting for dragons to return for a long time. Seeing you here gives some of them hope they didn't have before."

"But not you," I couldn't resist prodding.

He shrugged. "I haven't made up my mind yet."

Why should he, when all I'd been able to do was cringe in a corner yesterday while all our lives were in danger? I swallowed a grimace and turned to follow his gaze. Several of the villagers were still clustered together, glancing our way. Speculating about me?

Something felt off as I looked around. It took me several more seconds before I put my finger on it. "There aren't any kids. Or is there some rule about when they're allowed out of the house?" I hadn't seen anyone who looked younger than their mid-teens.

West's stance tensed. "There've been no shifter children born in sixteen years. At least not within the kin-groups. Kin can't conceive in their mate-pairs unless their alpha is mated. It's a biological block, to make sure vulnerable young aren't born into extremely troubled times."

"Oh." My eyes widened. "Because I—" Because Mom and I had been hidden away in New York, all the shifters had gone childless all this time. I glanced at West. He was still gazing into the common, his eyes even darker than usual. "*Could* you have taken a different mate? I don't know how all this stuff works yet."

"Yes," he said. "I still could. I could forsake the existing bond in order to form a new one. But once that's done, a shifter can never be mated to the one they gave up. You can't go back on the decision."

My stomach dropped. So all this time, despite all the doubts he'd had, he'd waited for me. Even though he'd had to watch his kin go without children.

Maybe I shouldn't have accused him of lacking loyalty.

"It... hasn't seemed like you'd have a problem with that outcome," I said tentatively.

West's gaze jerked back to me. "I *said* I haven't made up my mind." He rubbed his thumb over his palm, the scar there identical to the one Aaron had shown me. The mark of the alpha. "I knew you were alive, even if I didn't know where you were. I didn't think you'd stay away forever. It doesn't seem smart to throw away something without knowing what it is."

"I guess you do at least think I'm worth keeping alive," I said, tipping my head as if considering. "You fought the vampires to stop them from coming at me yesterday. I should probably thank you for that. So, thanks. I mean it."

"It was nothing," West said, his voice going gruff again. "No vampire is going to manage to hurt me. You *have* been making an awful lot of trouble, though."

"Yeah. I noticed. I'm sorry about that. None of this was in my life plan, you know."

"Of course not." He studied my face, some of the tension leaving his. For a second I thought he was going to add something. My pulse fluttered with the intensity of his attention. But he stayed quiet.

When the silence started to gnaw at me, I had to break it. "Do you really think the old traditions, with the dragon shifters and the alphas, could be wrong?"

He looked away, toward the buildings around us. "I don't know. I don't like how fragile that system turned out to be. One savage attack, and we nearly fell into chaos. If the rogues had caught you and your mother... I'm not saying it's definitely wrong. I just don't want to assume it's right. I have to be sure I'm doing the right thing for my kin before I take any steps I can't take back."

Well, if he'd put it that way to begin with, maybe I wouldn't have spent so much of the last two days pissed off at him. "Okay," I said. "That makes sense. I can respect that."

He shot me a look I could only describe as startled.

"What?" I said, setting my hands on my hips. "You didn't think I was capable of basic human empathy?"

The corners of his mouth twitched. "To be fair, you aren't actually human."

"Basic shifter empathy, then. I've gotten the impression we have that too."

"Some of the time, anyway." He kept his gaze on me. The energy between us had shifted somehow, with an electric prickling over my skin. His hand rose. I half expected him to reach for me, to pull me closer—

He made a dismissive gesture and stepped farther away. "I have a few more people to talk with while we're here in town," he said. "Try not to get into any *more* trouble, all right, Sparks?"

"I'll do my best," I muttered. Was I imagining things, or had that nickname sounded just slightly affectionate for the first time? It was hard to tell when he put on that gruff, no-nonsense voice.

West stalked off down the street. He must have said something to the people lingering in the common, because the group that had been watching me scattered. I rubbed my arms, feeling restless in the rising summer heat. And the heat that had started to rise inside me, standing next to him.

"It's good," a weathered voice said from behind me. As I turned, an elderly woman with a puff of frizzy white hair came up beside me. She patted my hand. "Matilda. Pleased to meet you, dragon shifter."

Her demeanor was so matter-of-fact after the awe I'd gotten from the other villagers that I immediately relaxed. "Pleased to meet you too, Matilda."

She turned her pale hazel eyes the way West had gone. "I'm glad Westley has finally found you," she said. "I can tell you'll be good for him."

*West*ley, huh? I let out a short laugh. "I'm not so sure he'd agree with you there."

"Aw, don't let his temper put you off. He's a good boy, even if he's slow to trust sometimes."

How long had she known him? Since he was a kid— or, what, a pup? And now he was running the whole kin-group. "You all seem to have a lot of respect for him," I said.

"He's earned it," Matilda said, and hummed softly as if to agree with herself. "That boy has always put his kin above everything else, even the folks he cared about the most."

That sounded like a story I needed to hear. But before I could push for details, Nate walked over. He gave the elder shifter a respectful bob of his head and turned to me.

"After last night, we're thinking giving you some self defense training might be a good idea, Ren. If you're up for it."

Anything if it meant I wasn't standing around like a hopeless damsel next time we got into a fight, as much as I hoped there wasn't a next time.

"Sure," I said. "Hit me."

Marco

MY PRINCESS of Flames wasn't going to be demolishing vampires by the end of the day, but it wasn't going to be long before she could hold her own either. She mimicked the motion of the punches Aaron demonstrated while Nate held up his broad hands as targets.

The bear shifter swept his leg toward her, and she nimbly leapt out of the way. Aaron caught her around the shoulders. She snapped his hold the way he'd taught her, grinning. The physical exertion had brought an incredibly appealing flush into her cheeks. I'd bet that whole lithe body of hers would be hot to the touch.

Kylie, West, and I formed an audience at the edge of the clearing on the outskirts of the village. Ren's human friend whistled and cheered. Wolf boy looked as if he'd eaten something sour, but that was pretty much his standard expression, so it was hard to read anything into it.

Ren had a ways to go yet, though. The guys were still being careful with her. I wasn't sure that was the best tack. Didn't they see what a firecracker that girl was? All that power in her just waiting to explode.

And when she got there, I'd be right at her side.

Aaron exchanged a couple of testing blows with Ren. She blocked and jabbed out with her fist, catching him in the ribs. "Good," he said. "Can you feel that fighting energy calling to your dragon? See if you can catch hold of the feeling and shift that form to the surface."

Ren nodded, her expression tightening with determination. Oh, princess, as if a shift was something you should have to force. She needed to make friends with her inner dragon, not battle it.

Nate stepped in, weaving back and forth with surprising speed for a guy that big. The bear wasn't all bulk. He pushed Ren backward until she ducked under one of his swings and darted around him. A fierce gleam lit in her eyes. Then she faltered. Her shoulders sagged, and she swiped her hand across her mouth.

"I'm trying," she said to Aaron. "I can feel it in there. I don't know why I'm so stuck still."

I ambled forward. "Maybe you need a different kind of provocation," I suggested.

She straightened up, the fire in her eyes coming back. "What did you have in mind?"

I rolled my shoulders, testing the limits of my shirt. The fabric had enough flexibility to stay comfortable. "Spar with me a bit, and you'll see."

Aaron gestured for me to go ahead and take over. "If you think you have a better idea, Marco…"

"Even if I don't, a little variety never hurt anyone." I shot him a grin and then turned it on Ren. "Let's go, princess."

We circled each other, Ren watching me warily. Waiting for me to make the first move so she could decide how to respond. Fine, I could play along. I feinted and took a controlled jab at her stomach. She dodged, smacking my arm to the side with a well-executed block. Then she dove at me, swinging her elbow at my ribs. I just barely leapt out of the way. Damn, the girl was fast when she wanted to be.

I moved closer, speeding up my own movements. A tap to the shoulder, a strike at her neck. And smaller gestures I gave enough concentration to that I could be sure they landed. A caress of her hip. A fleeting stroke of her side. I blocked her flying fist—and let my knuckles graze the peak of her breast.

Her breath caught, her cheeks flushing darker. She narrowed her eyes at me, as if to say she saw what I was doing. That was fine. I wanted her to feel it. To feel the desire that sparked hotter between us every time we touched.

If aggression didn't bring out her dragon, maybe passion would. And if it didn't, I was sure as hell enjoying trying.

It was probably obvious to our audience what I was doing by now, but I didn't care. She was my mate as much as any of the other alphas. They'd better get used to seeing her with me.

As she ducked low to block a kick, I took the opportunity to tease my fingertips over her cheek. She jerked up, throwing a punch. I bobbed out of the way and gave her ass a quick squeeze.

With a heated noise of frustration, she came at me swinging. I wove back and forth and then threw myself right back at her when she least expected it. She yelped as I tackled her to the ground. I pinned her on the grass, my body pressed against hers, my dick getting harder with each heave of her breath that shoved her breasts into my chest.

"Marco," she growled, glaring at me, but at the same time her hips canting welcomingly toward mine. There was as much lust as frustration in her eyes.

"Yes, princess?" I said sweetly. Before she could answer, I caught her mouth with a kiss.

Ren

Marco's kiss was as hot as the look he'd been giving me a second before. A shiver of pleasure rippled through me. God, did I want this man. I couldn't do anything except kiss him back just as hard.

He let go of my arm to trail his fingers down my side to my hip, and my hand leapt up to tangle in his hair. I yanked his mouth even tighter against mine. Marco hummed approvingly, nudging my lips apart with his demanding tongue. Mine slicked over his, tasting his mouth.

I could feel his pulse thumping in his chest, smell the spicy coffee scent of him, feel every shift and flex of his muscles as if I were all around him. The claws in my chest spread wide, reaching. The flavor of ash tainted the back of my mouth, but somehow that made the kiss even sweeter.

I nipped his lower lip—and tasted blood. My heartbeat raced faster. I wasn't just some girl for him to make out with. I was a *dragon*, and we were here to fight. I couldn't let him make me forget that.

With a strength I hadn't known I had in me, I shoved Marco off. He stumbled right onto his feet. A laugh jolted out of him, startled and impressed. Then I was springing after him, my feet barely seeming to touch the ground.

Marco's eyebrows rose as I lashed my arm out at him. The wind whistled strangely through my fingers.

Or rather, my talons. Scales had formed over my fingertips and sprouted dagger-like claws. *Yes.* A smile stretched across my face. I dashed faster, feeling the sinewy energy snaking through me, ready to break free.

Shouts carried across the field. "All right, Ren! You're amazing!" "Beautiful. Just give yourself over to the shift." "You've got this, Ren!"

The voices rattled my thoughts. I didn't have it, not yet. I needed more—I needed to *be* that dragon—

Even as I groped after the serpentine sensation inside me, it whipped away from me. I stumbled on the grass. My hands hit the ground, fully human again. I stared at them, those weak pale digits. My vision blurred. I blinked hard.

No. I was not going to cry. Not in front of the guys.

Even if I'd just proven myself an even bigger screw-up than before.

I'd been so fucking *close*.

I dug my fingers into the earth, clawing my disappointment into it the only way I could. A large form hunkered down beside me.

"It's fine," Nate said. "You're getting there. That was progress."

"He's right, princess," Marco said, standing a short distance away. "It'll take time to get full control over your powers, just like it'll take time for us to become full mates. And I promise I'm more impatient about the latter." He chuckled.

Nate shot him a frown and reached to rub my shoulder. "You should be proud of yourself."

Proud of myself? When I couldn't even manage to get halfway to what they all did so effortlessly?

I pulled away from him, scrambling to my feet. "I don't need coddling," I said. "I need to figure this out."

Aaron ambled over to join us. West and Kylie had hung back, my friend looking concerned but uncertain. This was one challenge she couldn't meet with me.

"I think you're pushing yourself too hard," Aaron said in his mild voice. The evenness of it, paired with that faint rasp, seemed to file down the sharp edges of my emotions. "I know some mental exercises that might help with that for the next time you try. You could take a break, and then—"

"No break," I interrupted. "If you've got something to teach me that might help, let's do it now."

He paused, but then he nodded. "All right." He

glanced around at the others. "We'll need to be undisturbed for this."

Marco saluted him. "Enjoy your mind games, eagle boy."

Nate drew back, his expression worried. I didn't know what to say to him to make him feel better. My sense of failure jabbed deeper into my chest. I turned to Aaron. "Let's go."

He motioned for me to follow him. At the edge of the clearing, close to the village's nearest buildings, a circle of beech trees formed a small, sheltered glade. We squeezed between them. Aaron sat down cross-legged in their midst, so I copied him, sitting across from him.

"Is this some kind of mediation you want me to do?" I asked.

"Something like that. To begin with, you could focus on your breathing. Feel it traveling into and out of your lungs. Let it fill your chest fully before you expel it. Get a sense of control over it, and of how by moderating it, you can moderate your emotions."

Apparently he could tell that my emotions were in severe need of moderation. I sucked in a breath, shaky with frustration. My hands balled at my sides. No, that definitely didn't fit the exercise. I had to give this a real try.

Maybe there wasn't some artificial block inside me that was keeping me from my dragon. Maybe *I* was the one holding it in, holding myself too tight and tense around it.

I inhaled more slowly, letting the air flow into my lungs. My ribs expanded. The breath shuddered on the way out, and I gritted my teeth. Why couldn't I get even this right?

"Hey," Aaron said gently. "Come here?"

He beckoned me over. I swiveled and scooted backward so I could lean against his folded legs. He set his hands on my upper arms, his thumbs tracing light arcs over my biceps. The warmth of his presence soaked into my back, even though there was at least a foot between our bodies. That bond, that tug. The tie that marked us as mates. I wet my lips, trying to push aside the swell of desire.

"This isn't something anyone masters on their first try," Aaron said. "Relaxing is one of the hardest things someone like us has to do. Try again? In and out, slow and easy. Focus on the feeling of my hands, and try to let any other thoughts wisp right by you."

His thumbs continued their careful arc back and forth over my skin. The thoughts they were provoking were a totally different kind of frustration from before. But I followed his instructions, closing my eyes. In and out. Like the to and fro of his caress. Slow and even. Nothing else needed to matter except for that and the heat of his touch.

Another breath slipped from my lungs, and I realized I was doing it. The tension had seeped out of me. Disappointment no longer ached behind my sternum. I didn't know if this was going to help me bring forth my dragon, but it definitely hadn't hurt anything.

"Thanks," I said. "I guess I needed that."

I heard Aaron's smile in the shape of his voice. "Sometimes we shifters can get too caught up in the animal side of our natures. I think it's important to remember we're so much more than that. Our minds matter too. As enjoyable as certain animalistic impulses might be."

A little mischief crept into his tone with that last sentence. I shot him a glance over my shoulder, and the slightly wicked smile he gave me then sent a wash of heat over me. So my Disney prince had a bit of an edge to him, did he?

The attraction burning between us loosened a memory—one from not that long ago. "Marco said something... He said in time we'd become 'full mates.' I thought we were already mates. Is there something else we need to *do*...?"

Aaron's smile turned wry. "There's no hurry," he said. "You shouldn't take that step until you're fully comfortable with the idea, with each of us. The mate-bond isn't confirmed until it's consummated—that is, until the mates—"

"—have sex," I filled in for him. "Ah." My cheeks flared. "Yeah, I'm not sure how long it's going to take before I'm ready for that. I... never have before."

Because that wrenching, clawing feeling had always gotten in the way before. But I didn't feel that with any of the alphas. I wanted to open myself up to them. At least, I thought I did. There'd been so many upheavals and revelations in the last couple days—how could I really be sure what I wanted? What was best for me?

What was best for *them*?

"You knew you were bonded without even understanding it," Aaron said. His hands smoothed over my shirt to lightly massage my back. "It's possible to be intimate with someone you're not bonded too, but part of you is always going to balk. I won't pretend I haven't had desires and pursued them, to some extent, but the same feeling always held me back. Being that close with anyone else just didn't feel right."

So it wasn't just me. The guys felt it too? I glanced back at him again, with a fluttering in my chest. I'd waited for them without knowing what I was doing. And he'd waited for me too.

"There really isn't any rush to make that commitment," he said, gazing back at me with those clear blue eyes. "We've only just found you. We can give you whatever time you need."

Not everyone felt that way. My thoughts darted to West's words earlier this morning. It must be the same for all of the kin-groups, including Aaron's. The longer I held out, leaving him without a mate, the longer the rest of his kin had to go barren.

"Are you sure?" I asked before I knew I was going to. "I mean, that waiting for me is the right decision? What if..."

My voice faltered. My doubts jumbled awkwardly inside me.

Aaron leaned forward and wrapped his arms around me, tipping his face next to mine. "I've never been more sure of anything, Serenity. You're everything I could have wanted in a mate."

My back tensed against his chest. He drew back a few inches. "You don't like people using your full name, do you?"

I grimaced. "It's not so much that as—I just got so used to pretending it wasn't my name. To feeling like saying it would be a dangerous thing."

"Just one more thing you need to reclaim," he murmured. "You are Serenity Drake. You are the last in the dragon shifter line. That heritage belongs to you and no one else. No one can take it from you."

He pressed a kiss to the sensitive spot just behind my ear. A bolt of desire shot through me, right to my sex. I pushed myself toward him, and he eased me onto his lap. When I raised my head, his lips were right there to meet mine.

We kissed until I started to lose my breath. Aaron edged his thumb under the hem of my tee. I mumbled encouragingly, and he slid his hand right up under, over my bare skin. He teased his knuckles over my breast, making my nipple pebble. I moaned, kissing him harder. A tight ball of need formed between my legs.

Carefully, he eased the strap of my bra over my shoulder to loosen it. Then he dipped his fingers inside the cup to fondle me skin to skin. I gasped as he rolled my nipple under his thumb, drawing it to an even sharper peak. He bent his head and nibbled his way down my neck.

Every nerve in my body hummed at his touch. I was getting carried away again, but it didn't feel quite so scary. I could do this. I could take this pleasure. And if I wanted to stop, I knew all I had to do was say so.

I shoved my hands up under Aaron's shirt, needing to feel the hot, firm planes of his chest. All that coiled strength. I traced the lines of those muscles all the way down to the waist of his pants. Aaron groaned, squeezing my breast. His erection pressed against my thigh. So big and so *hard*, all for me.

The thought sent a flare of hunger through me, but it came with an icy splinter of panic.

I could have him. Tie him to me so he was mine for the rest of my life. If I said I was ready now, that I wanted all of him, he wouldn't hesitate. He'd give himself over just like that, for all time. To a shifter who couldn't even shift, a dragon who couldn't sprout her own wings.

I pulled back, my head dropping. Aaron's hand stilled. "Far enough?"

I dragged in a breath to steady myself. The hunger still gnawed at me. My lips ached to feel his against them.

"Far enough," I agreed. "But... we can stay here for a while."

He grinned and brought his mouth back to mine.

CHAPTER 16

Ren

"Wow," Kylie said, hugging my arm. "Shifters know how to eat, don't they?"

We were standing at one end of the huge table that had been set up in the village common. It stretched across the entire space, and even then it wasn't enough for all the villagers to sit down. Many were filling their plates from the bowls and platters set all down the middle and ambling off to find a spot on the ground or the extra chairs scattered around the common.

Delicious smells assaulted my nose: roasted meat and stewed veggies and fresh bread. I wasn't drooling, but it was a near thing. Between working out and making out, I'd developed a healthy appetite for dinner. I grabbed one of the plates.

"I don't think they do this all the time," I said.

"Obviously." Kylie rolled her eyes. "It's all for you. You're a celebrity!"

She said it teasingly, but the fact was it was kind of true. Every shifter we passed gave me a longer look than they aimed at anyone else. Several of the cooks dashed over to encourage me to try this casserole or those ribs. When we made for a couple of chairs off to the side, a middle-aged man stopped us and motioned us back to the table.

"No, no, you have a spot here, of course," he said, dipping his head. "There's always room for you at our table."

I looked for my alphas, hoping one of them might step in and tell everyone to stop fussing, I wasn't that big a deal. But then, they kind of thought I was a big deal too, didn't they? West was busy stalking through the crowd, offering a greeting here and a friendly slap to the shoulder there. Marco was chatting with a few rather roguish-looking guys. Nate and Aaron had paused to talk down by the other end of the table. No help from any of them.

More of the villagers came around as I ate. As soon as I'd tried one thing off my plate, someone had brought me two more tidbits. They watched me eagerly, so I did my best to try everything, but before too long my stomach was protesting from being stuffed and from the pressure.

"What do you say we take a little stroll and walk off some of this feast?" I said to Kylie.

She nodded. "Yeah, I can see a breather might be a good idea. Being famous is hard."

She elbowed me playfully as we stood up, but she cleared the way through the crowd, giving our excuses. "Just taking a little walk. We'll be back soon!"

We ducked between a couple of shops that had closed for the evening, hurried past a short line of houses, and rambled out along the edge of the tree-spotted hills that surrounded most of the town. As soon as the sounds of the feast had faded behind me, I exhaled in relief. Kylie linked her arm around mine.

"It's weird, yeah?" she said.

"*So* weird." I laughed, glad there was one person here who understood that. I might be a shifter by birth, but after all those years in the city, living like and believing I was only human, I didn't belong here. Not really.

"But hey, at least that weirdness comes with four super-devoted and extra-super-hot guys."

I gave her a little shove. "Three devoted guys and one who's not sure I deserve the time of day."

She snickered. "Oh, no. I've seen the way the Big Bad Wolf looks at you."

"We're still bonded," I muttered. "He can't help feeling something. That doesn't mean he wants it to stay that way."

"Oh, so you might only have three super-hot mates? I guess you'll survive somehow. When you're queen of all shifters, maybe you can find some extras to send my way?"

"You'd really want that?" Kylie hooked up with guys now and then when she was in the mood, but she'd never seemed all that boy crazy.

She shrugged. "Why not? If they look like that and worship the ground I walk on, I don't see how it could go wrong."

"I don't know. You could find out that the entire future of the shifters depends on you. I was only just getting used to the responsibility of having rent to pay." I glanced back toward the common, hidden beyond the houses. "All those people think I'm going to *save* them somehow."

"Okay, I can see how that would be a bit much." Kylie dropped her hand to squeeze mine. "You don't *have* to do it, right? I mean, your wolfman is always going on about having a choice and making his own decisions. You get to do that too. If you really don't think you're up for the whole shifter queen gig, couldn't you tell them you're out, that they should go find some other mate?"

I paused. I hadn't really considered that possibility before. "I guess so. But then the kin-groups will be on their own, nothing uniting them. From what they've said, it's always been the dragon shifter doing that. And I'm the only one around." Maybe the only one at all.

What would have happened if my older sisters had survived? Would I have taken on this role at all, or just watched from the sidelines? I hadn't thought to ask that before, but now the question itched at me. I'd have to ask the guys the next time I had the chance.

Kylie waved her free hand in the air. "I'm just saying, you didn't sign up for this. It's your life too. Maybe when you find your mom, she'll be able to help you figure things out."

"*If* I find my mom. I still have no idea why she sent me down into that subway tunnel." I dipped my hand into my purse and tugged out the crystal slab. It was the closest thing I had to a connection to Mom, so I'd been keeping it with me. But looking at its glossy surface only made me more annoyed. "Why couldn't she at least have left me a note or something telling me what the hell I'm supposed to do with this?"

Had she meant to tell me more? Thinking back to the voice I'd heard in my head, she'd stopped so abruptly... Because that'd been all she had to say, or because she'd been interrupted? Maybe she'd had to tangle with vampires down there too.

Maybe she hadn't made it past them, without a squad of alphas to fight beside her.

No. I couldn't think like that.

I turned the circle, watching the light play off its faintly etched surface. "Let me see?" Kylie said. I handed it to her, and she held it up over her head as if examining the sky through it. She wrinkled her nose and passed it back to me. "Nope. Still not getting it. It's a really nice piece of abstract art, though." She waggled her fingers over it. "Maybe you need a little voodoo to activate—"

I registered the moving shadow from the corner of my eye only an instant before a black-furred wolf leapt out of it. That instant saved my life. The wolf lunged straight for my throat, and my reflexes kicked in just soon enough to spin sideways.

The beast hit my shoulder instead, teeth raking my flesh though my shirt sleeve, paws pummeling me to the ground. Pain splintered through my arm. With a gasp, I lashed out with the only thing close to a weapon I had on me—the crystal slab in my hand. I smacked it into the wolf's skull.

The creature jerked back a few inches, blood dribbling from its mouth. With a snarl, it smashed its paw against the slab. The thick crystal didn't break, but it jolted from my clutching fingers and tumbled across the grass.

A blur of motion whipped past me. Kylie shrieked. I caught a glimpse of flailing arms and two gray-furred bodies looming over her. Then the wolf snapped at me again. I kicked at its heavy body, slammed my elbow into its jaw, and screamed with all the panic and pain rushing through me.

"Help! Somebody help us!"

The wolf cuffed me across the temple, growling. My head spun. I jabbed out with all my limbs. As long as I kept moving, as long as I kept fighting back, I had a chance. It sank its teeth into my blocking forearm, and a sharper pain radiated through my flesh. A whimper broke from my throat. I kneed at the creature's belly, but I couldn't budge it. It scraped its claws across my abdomen with another sear of agony.

Where were those goddamned talons I'd managed to sprout this morning? If I could just shift into the scaled, fire-breathing animal I knew I had in me, I'd show this beast what real hurting was.

But the scrabbling inside me felt more desperate than determined. Every time I tried to reach for the power inside me, the wolf wrenched at my arm or gouged its claws into me again. I couldn't focus on anything through the haze of pain.

Shouts rang out. The wolf flinched. It took one last bite at my throat, but I managed to knock its muzzle to the side with my throbbing arm. The stink of its rasping breath flooded my nose as its fangs nicked my chin. Then it was springing away.

A thunder of rushing paws echoed around me. A whole pack of wolves shot past me, snarling and snapping at the fleeing animals.

My whole body was on fire—and not the enjoyable kind. I rolled onto my side, toward Kylie. My shredded shirt tugged at my wounds, tacky with blood. More streaked down the hand I reached toward my best friend.

Kylie was sprawled in the grass, her face turned away from me, her arm twisted at an unnatural angle behind her. Her pink pixie-cut was streaked with red.

My fault. I hadn't protected her. I hadn't even been able to protect myself.

A few of the running bodies shifted back into human form around us. Nate's warm hand pressed against my side. "Ren! Quick, we've got to stop the bleeding."

Aaron pressed a folded shirt to my side. The sting expanded, and I shuddered. "You'll be okay," he said. "You're already healing. Dragons heal fast." But even his mild voice came out ragged.

"Kylie," I said. Marco dropped onto his knees beside me and clasped my hand to stop me from moving my arm any more than I already had. Four women had clustered around my friend. One scratched her own wrist with her teeth and dribbled blood over Kylie's wounds. The others pressed bandages over them.

"She's alive," one of them said, catching my gaze. "We'll make sure she stays that way. No rogue will take a life on our watch. I'll empty my own body of blood before I let that happen."

Alive. Kylie was alive. A small shiver of relief passed through me. Not enough to dislodge the knot of guilt in my stomach, but I finally let myself sag into the grass.

Aaron was right. A splintering heat was crawling up to my skin from inside me now, knitting my flesh back together. At least that part of my shifter powers didn't need me to coax it into working.

The sensation hurt almost as bad as getting the wounds in the first place. My eyelids drooped as exhaustion rolled through me with it.

"What did they do to her?" a voice said from over me. Was that West? I'd never heard *him* sound so pained.

"Bit and scratched her up, but nothing too deep for her to heal on her own," Aaron said. "They were clearly trying to do a lot worse. Did you catch any of them?"

"Not exactly." West spat out the words. "A few of the others pounced on one of the coyotes, but they didn't stop to ask questions. And he's never going to be answering any now. The others took off too fast. Rogues."

"They all looked like canine-kin," Nate remarked.

"They *aren't* my kin," West snapped. "No matter what they look like."

"Of course the rogue group would send canines for

an attack here," Aaron said. "They'd have been hoping you wouldn't smell them approaching, since they'd blend in with the locals." He smoothed his hand over my hair. I opened my eyes, and he gave me a tight smile. "Good thing we started on the self-defense lessons."

"I couldn't get it off me," I murmured, my throat hoarse. "I tried—I couldn't stop them—"

"Hey," Nate said. "You stopped them from *killing* you. That's all that matters."

Marco straightened up. "So they already know we're here. That's a pity. We'll have to assume they're following our movements from now on."

Were we going to move? I didn't want to go anywhere. I didn't want the guys to go. If they left...

My thoughts jumbled in my head. I ached too much to set them straight. I tipped my head, and my gaze caught on the crystal slab.

It was sitting in the grass, leaning against a rock where it had fallen. A splash of blood had splattered across its clear face. Splattered and seeped darker into the lines and dots of the etching. I stared at it, my vision doubling and steadying again as my body throbbed. A memory rippled past my eyes.

Mom, perched at our dining room table. Pouring over a map on her tablet. I'd glanced over her shoulder as I'd walked by, and she'd tapped the app closed.

What are you looking at? I'd asked her, and she'd said, *Nothing for you to worry about.* And two days later, she'd vanished.

The lines and speckles—I hadn't seen their exact pattern before, but I'd seen patterns like them. They were laid out like a map's roads, rivers, and towns. They'd looked so random before, but now, at that angle, with them drawn so starkly in my blood, the full picture swam into focus.

Follow the crystal. The damned thing was literally a map.

CHAPTER 17

Ren

"Are you sure that's the right place?" West said, frowning at my phone. I'd set it in the middle of the table between the five of us with the map app open.

"Look at it," I said, motioning between it and the crystal slab. "They're practically identical. I poured over the entire country, and that's the only place that's even close."

Aaron eased the phone a little closer to him to study it. "Sunridge, Wyoming. Do you have any idea why your mother would have wanted you to go there?"

"Or why there'd be a lovely picture of it imprinted on a crystal in the first place?" Marco remarked.

I shook my head. The muscles in my shoulder stung at the movement. I'd kept healing as I slept last night, but ruddy marks still streaked my arm, chest, and abdomen where the wolf had sliced me up. The pain hadn't completely eased either.

"I've never heard of it," I said. "Mom never mentioned it. But why would she send me to find the crystal if she didn't want me to go to the place it shows?"

"We can make the drive," Nate said. "Even stopping for the night, we'd get there tomorrow. We can figure out the rest once we see what's there."

"As much as I enjoy a good adventure," Marco said, "I'm feeling weary of surprises at the moment. I say we don't leave until wolf boy's people are finished their patrol."

He glanced at West, who gave him a short nod. "They're still surveying the area around the village for any further signs of rogue activity. I expect them to report back within the next couple hours."

"So we're sticking around here until then?" I said. "In that case, I want to get in some more defense training."

Aaron's eyebrows rose slightly. "You're still recovering. You shouldn't strain your body too much."

I pushed back my chair. "I'm not saying we go all out. But I need to be able to handle myself better in a fight. These guys are obviously still after me. That attack won't be the last one. I want to know I can get through the next time on more than just luck."

"Ren," Nate started, but West glowered at him.

"She wants to train. She says she can handle it. Is she a dragon or not?"

Good question. My gaze darted to the ceiling. Kylie was lying in one of the bedrooms upstairs, resting from injuries she didn't have the supernatural ability to quickly heal. It wasn't just my own life at stake.

"I guess I'll just fight West if none of the rest of you wants to come," I said. West narrowed his eyes at me when I shot him a challenging smile.

In the end, all five of us tramped back into the clearing where we'd practiced yesterday morning. A few of the villagers trailed after us, but to my relief West spoke to them and they drifted away. I shifted my weight from one foot to the other, jitters running through my muscles.

I was way too wound up. That hadn't helped me any yesterday. Thinking back to my little interlude with Aaron—the part before I'd gotten distracted by his hands and his lips—I inhaled slowly and felt my lungs expand. In and out. Steady and even. I'd spent so much time hiding myself away, not even knowing why, but now it was safe for me to let my dragon out. Now I *needed* to.

Those rogue shifters who'd attacked me last night, they hadn't cared that I couldn't fully access my powers yet. They'd seen me as a threat anyway. Anger stirred in my chest at the thought, along with a shudder of energy like the flap of powerful wings. I could be that threat. I had it in me—I knew I did.

"When you're attacked by someone stronger than you, there's no shame in taking every advantage you can get," Aaron said. He pointed to his own body. "We all have weak spots where one quick hit can do a lot of damage. Eyes. Throat. Groin. If you can get a strike in any of those places, go for it."

"But maybe not while you're sparring with us,"

Marco piped up. "I'd personally like to keep the family jewels unsmashed."

Nate rolled his eyes at the jaguar shifter. "Not helpful, Marco." He glanced at Aaron. "Maybe we could find her a weapon she can get comfortable with, for the time being."

"And break shifter law?" West shook his head. "Are you out of your mind? I thought the whole point of bringing her back into the fold was to settle everyone down, not rile them up even more."

"There's a law against us using weapons?" I said.

Aaron nodded. "The kin-groups decided together that no shifter should attack another with anything but their own strength. Our strength we inherit and earn; winning that kind of fight is a fair measure of victory. It also means most of the time no one has to die over a scuffle."

"But she can't use all of her strength yet," Nate said. "If there's ever been a time to make an exception—"

"No," I said quickly. I didn't want any more exceptions made for me. "I've got to learn to do this the shifter way. Come on. Who's going to try me?"

Marco stepped forward with his crooked grin. I waved a finger at him. "No funny business this time."

"I don't know if I'd have called what we were getting up to yesterday *funny*," he drawled. Amusement and heat mixed in his gaze. The memory of our kiss stirred the embers of desire inside me. I swallowed and raised my hands defensively.

That desire had worked in my favor yesterday. If there was some way I could combine that with Aaron's clear-headedness and my anger at last night's attackers...

Marco came at me with a quick feint and a swing of his fist. I dodged to the side and managed to land a kick to his knee. "Oh, you're not getting away with that," he said, his indigo eyes gleaming, and caught me around the waist. I managed to yank out of his arms, spinning around, my heart beating faster.

As he circled me, I reached back to last night's assault. The searing of the rogue wolf's teeth and claws slashing into my flesh. They couldn't have sliced into scales. I could have towered over him, set him aflame.

Next time I would. Next time.

I held onto that thought, whipping a fist toward Marco and darting out of his reach. Tension started to tighten my chest, but I breathed into it, willing it to release. I wasn't going to force my dragon. I was going to let it come over me naturally. Because it was who I was. Because those beasts had threatened me and the people I cared about, and I was *not* going to let that stand.

From the corner of my eye, I saw Aaron motion to Nate. "Let's mix things up a bit." Nate shucked off his clothes in a couple of smooth movements. Before I'd quite processed what was happening, he was loping toward me in bear form. Marco veered to the side, chuckling under his breath.

Nate bared his teeth at me, but his grizzly face managed to look apologetic at the same time. "It's fine," I said to him. "Come and get me."

He bounded closer and loomed over me on his rear legs. One enormous paw swung at my head.

I ducked under it, my pulse racing through my veins. The gleam of claws and the massive animalistic presence brought back more flashes of last night. And more of last night's terror. The sealed cuts on my arms and torso prickled.

I was stronger than that. I *was*. I threw myself at Nate's furred legs, trying to tip him off-balance. He swayed and dropped down over me, but I rolled to the side just in time. My feet seemed to bite into the ground as I shoved myself upright. Power coiled through my thighs. An ashen taste crept up my throat.

Yes. He lunged at me, and I leapt to the side, faster than before. My haunches were bunching and expanding, unused muscles unfurling their strength. The armor of scales tingled over my skin from knees to waist. An itch formed in the middle of my back where my wings should form.

Let it come. Let it come. But as the sensation swept higher, my lungs expanding, a jolt of panic shot through me.

What was I doing? I couldn't control it, couldn't feel where it would stop.

I'd lost so goddamn much. I couldn't lose myself too.

The thoughts didn't make much sense, but they jarred against my shift. I stumbled and fell to my knees. Knees that were pale and human, peeking through the tears in my sweatpants.

I *had* started to shift. My pants were hanging right off me where my legs had swelled to closer to dragon size. I grasped the tatters, peering at the skin beneath as if I could will the scales to return.

I'd gotten closer. So close I could still taste the fire in the back of my mouth.

"You know, Sparks, I'm starting to think *you* want this to work less than anyone," West said from the edge of the clearing. My head jerked up, my cheeks flaming.

Nate growled, shifting back into human form as he strode toward West. "Could you shut up for once?" he snapped. "I'd like to see how well you handled the shift if you'd gone sixteen years without the chance to try."

"Nate," Aaron said, and the bigger guy halted. The eagle-shifter turned to West. "I agree with him, though. If you're going to just stand there griping, we don't need you here."

West scowled. The tension in the air wrenched at me. This was my fault too, the clashing between the alphas. Because I couldn't do the thing I'd been born to do. Damn it!

Marco cocked his head. "Company arriving," he said. "Come here, princess."

He offered his hand to help me up. I clutched at my ruined pants, holding the larger scraps of fabric over my crotch. Marco smirked, leaning in for a second as I stood. "Nothing I won't see soon enough." His sly voice sent a shiver of anticipation through me despite my churning emotions.

A squad of shifters appeared at the edge of the clearing. West's people—I was learning to read the signs. Canine shifters tended toward the lean and lanky, cool and wary. The red-headed one who looked like she was barely twenty-one herself I'd bet was a fox.

West stalked over to meet them. "Report?" he said.

"No sign of the rogues in a twenty-mile radius," the man at the fore of the group said. "We didn't even scent them. However they got here, they're gone now."

"Not too far gone, I'm sure," West muttered. He turned back toward the rest of us. "If we're going, we should get out of here while we know the immediate area is clear. Less chance that they'll be watching closely enough to see where we're headed. I want to hear the details, and then I'll be ready to go. Sparks, get some new pants in the meantime."

My bag packed and my legs re-covered by pants I hadn't mangled, I went in to see Kylie alone.

She was sitting up on the bed, her back propped against a pillow, skimming her thumb over her phone's screen. Thick bandages lay across her neck and her right arm, and those were only the ones I could see. A purple bruise marked her forehead. Our shifter hosts had washed the blood from her hair, but the pink tufts still lay more limply than usual. But she smiled when she saw me and set down the phone.

"Time to go?" she said.

"Yeah." I hesitated. "I don't want to just leave you here with a bunch of strangers, but we don't know if the rogues will attack again when we're—"

"Oh, Ren." She held out her arms, beckoning me over. I walked into her embrace. I hugged her carefully, worried about her injuries, but she squeezed me with all her strength. "Don't worry about me. These people are looking after me just fine. You've got your stuff to do. I'll hang out a while longer, and Aaron said it should be okay for me to go back to the city by the time I'm all fixed up. You just have to promise you'll come visit me even if you get all busy with shifter queen business, you hear?"

A pained smile tugged at my lips. "Of course. You're still my best friend."

"That's right. Besties for life." She let go of me to raise her hand, and we tapped knuckles. "Don't get too distracted by all those yummy men either, okay? But you'd better indulge at least a little."

A blush tickled up the back of my neck. "I think I've already got that covered."

"Oh ho! Something else I'm going to need to hear all about." She gave my arm one last pat and waved me off. "Focus on finding your mom. I want to hear all about the end of that mystery too."

"I hope it's a good one," I said with total honesty. What was waiting for us in Sunridge, Wyoming? Another clue to another branch of this weird scavenger hunt Mom had sent us on, or some actual answers this time?

Was *Mom* waiting there? I didn't know what I'd say if I finally saw her again, but God, I wanted to so badly.

"Go," Kylie said, outright shooing me now. "Don't let me hold you back."

The guys were standing around the eight-seater SUV West had commandeered, as I guessed you could do when you were an alpha. The idea was that we could sleep in it overnight rather than going through the hassle of finding a hotel. And I suspected the guys liked having the extra space rather than being squashed into a regular car.

I tossed my bag in the trunk, and Nate yanked the hatch shut. Without any debate—or maybe I'd missed one—West climbed into the driver's seat. Aaron got in beside him. He'd been studying the maps.

As Marco nabbed a spot in the middle row, Nate closed his solid, warm hand around mine. It was funny: Even though I'd seen him in his animal form more often than any of the other guys, and even though that form was the most menacing of the four, his presence wasn't anything but comforting. Well, and maybe a little exciting. My gaze lingered on the muscles that filled out his thin tee, and a headier warmth pooled low in my belly.

He tugged me with him toward the backseat, and I came without argument. When we sat down on the soft leather, he wrapped his arm around me and tipped me against his brawny torso. I breathed in the musky, peppery smell of him. So fucking delicious. There were a lot of things screwed up about the situation I'd found myself in, but having these four guys by my side... at least, the three of them who definitely wanted to be there... might make up for the rest.

The car's engine rumbled. Its vibration hummed faintly through the seats as West turned us toward the road out of town. I let my head lean against Nate's broad shoulder.

I didn't want to think right now—not about Kylie's injuries or having to leave her behind, not about the rogues who'd tracked me down to kill me just two days after I'd found out who I really was, not about the quest my mother had sent me on. Drowning in Nate's scent and the feel of his body sounded like heaven. If I lifted my face just a couple inches, I could have pressed my lips to the base of his collarbone just above the neck of his shirt and tasted him too.

But I held myself back. The other guys were right *there*. Obviously they had to know I felt this connection to all of them, but I wasn't the biggest fan of PDAs. And anyway, I wasn't sure I deserved to indulge after yet another failure this morning.

Nate's hand rubbed up and down my arm. "You're tense," he murmured. "Is there anything you want to talk about?"

"No," I said automatically, but maybe there was. "I just—I hate that I seem to have that block when it comes to shifting. If I could have shifted last night, I'd have destroyed those rogue shifters."

He smiled. "You absolutely would have, Ren. But you don't have to worry about that. You've got all of us. We're not going to let anyone get that close to you again. We should have been more careful to begin with—I didn't realize they'd be brazen enough to attack you that close to a kin settlement."

Shit, he'd better not be feeling guilty. "It's not your fault," I said. "And I know you all want to protect me. But *I* want to be able to defend myself, like I should be able to."

"And you will." He brushed his lips against the top of my head. The contact sent a tingle over my scalp. "You're comparing yourself to the four of us, and we've had decades to grow into our powers. I'm *impressed* by how quickly you're discovering yourself."

"Oh." He sounded like he meant it. Was I being too hard on myself? I found it difficult to believe, but the knot of guilt inside me loosened just a little.

I nestled closer to him. He lifted my legs onto his lap so I was completely cuddled against him. My great teddy bear of a man. His other hand kept up its caresses up and down my arm—and reached a little farther to graze the side of my breast. I swallowed a gasp, arching into the contact instinctively. Correction, my great *hot* bear of a man.

Nate ducked his head to nip my earlobe. My heart skipped giddily. "I think you deserve a reward for all your hard work," he said under his breath, a playful note slipping into his voice.

"What do you have in mind?" I whispered back.

"You seem to be enjoying this." He traced his fingertips over the curve of my breast again, catching the peak this time. I clamped my mouth shut against a whimper.

"The other guys..."

"Won't mind at all. We belong to you, Ren. Whatever you need. Whatever you want."

His answer brought back Kylie's comment in the subway tunnel, about being with the guys at the same time. Nate kissed the side of my neck with a teasing swipe of tongue, and suddenly I was wondering what it would be like to have one of my other alpha's hands on me at the same time. Stirring up even more of these heady sensations. Driving me wild.

The thought dampened my panties. Nate cupped my breast, his thumb easing back and forth over my hardened nipple. Shivers of pleasure raced through me. There wasn't anything in the world I wanted more in that moment than to keep feeling what I was feeling right now. One last hesitation held me from completely giving in.

"I don't think I'm ready yet. I mean, to—"

"Ren," Nate murmured. My name in his low, longing baritone sent a flush over my skin. "You don't need to do anything. Let me just do this for you."

His free hand traveled up my thigh. He eased it up and down, still caressing my breast while he did, until the heat building inside me had me ready to melt. I flexed my hips, and he dipped his fingers between my legs to meet the spot so desperate for contact.

My whole body caught fire as he stroked my core. He teased his fingers over every sensitive part of me as if he knew exactly what I was hungry to feel. Pleasure sparked through my veins. I gripped his shirt, my breath growing shaky. I was melting together and coming apart all at once.

Nate flicked his thumb over my clit. I barely managed to bite back a moan. My hips moved to match his rhythm. "That's right," he said softly. "I've got you."

Oh, he did. He angled his mouth to capture mine, drinking in my whimper as his hand slid up to delve right under my clothes. He slicked a finger over my opening. The heel of his hand swiveled against my clit. A wave of bliss swelled inside me, tingling through my body from head to toe. I kissed him back as if I were starving for it, my fingers curling tighter into his shirt.

He pumped his hand gently. Then his rhythm started to speed up. I shuddered against him, so close to the edge, and he hooked his finger right up inside me.

The damn broke. Pleasure rushed through me like a flash fire, consuming my bones and leaving my muscles quivering.

Nate kept stroking me until the last waves of my orgasm had faded. He kissed me again, sweet but demanding, and tucked me against him as if I was meant to fit right there in his arms. I held onto him, momentarily sated.

Wondering how on earth I could possibly deserve this much devotion.

CHAPTER 18

West

ONE DEER'S trail smelled a little fresher than the others. That one had fallen behind the herd. From its scent, it was full-grown but young. Probably injured then. Some stumble that had lamed it and made it easier prey.

I stalked after it, the leaves of the forest underbrush rippling over my fur. Everything I needed for hunting was sharper in my wolf form: my nose, my claws, my teeth. It felt good to flex those muscles after all that time cooped up in the car. No living thing should spend an entire day on the road in one of those metal boxes.

As I wove through the forest, I tasted the air for other scents. The world was full of pungent sap and loamy moss. But what I was really watching for was the cloying sugary sweetness of the fae.

I hadn't caught a trace of it so far, but you couldn't be too careful when you ventured into the wilderness. The untamed stretches of countryside were as much fae territory as the human cities belonged to the bloodsuckers. The magic-burned scar on my upper chest prickled at the thought.

The only sweetness in the air now was a faint wisp from back at our camp. The tart honeyed scent that belonged to Ren. It tugged at me, even from that distance. Reminding me I was meant to be there with her. As if hunting for dinner wasn't a suitably mately duty. But that tug wouldn't ease off until I claimed her.

Or disowned her.

That thought brought back the expression on her face yesterday morning, when I'd told her how easily I could cast aside our bond if I decided to. It'd hurt her, hearing that, if just for a moment. But she'd still been able to tell me she respected my position. She hadn't pleaded or argued. She'd believed that I would do what I felt to be right, and that it was my right to do so.

Maybe I'd been too harsh with her, the last few days. *She* hadn't really run. And it definitely hadn't been her choice to hide. If I was going to be angry with anyone for the situation we found ourselves in, it should be her mother.

I didn't enjoy causing Ren pain. And when I remembered her agonized breath as she'd lain bloody in the grass last night—

My chest tightened. That was exactly why she needed someone to be harsh. She had to learn to withstand whatever got thrown at her. Because our enemies were going to be so much harsher than I'd ever stoop to.

The deer's scent grew thicker. I was almost on it. I slowed to a prowl, my ears perked. Hooves pattered in the brush. Unevenly, one leg holding it back with a limp. Just as I'd guessed.

My muscles bunched. I bolted forward and sprang. My jaws clamped around the deer's sleek neck.

With one snap, I severed its throat. A hot gush of fresh blood filled my mouth. The deer squealed, but its body was already sagging. By the time its head hit the ground, the poor beast had slumped completely, all the life gone from it.

My wolfish heart thumped with glee and the longing to dig in. But I wasn't hunting just for me. It'd be easier to carry the kill back to camp in human form.

I shifted, reveling in the smooth transition of muscle and bone from one form to the other. I was never more sure of myself and who I was meant to be than in those moments. With the back of my hand, I wiped the lingering blood from my mouth. Not a great look in man form. I lifted the deer, let the worst of the flow drain from its neck, and then hefted the slack body over my shoulder.

I'd left my clothes in a heap just beyond the grove at the side of the road, where we'd parked the van. I set down the deer and pulled them on before moving to join the others. I had nothing to hide, but I didn't want to have to explain the strange scar to Ren. And she wasn't exactly used to having people stroll around naked in front of her ye. The heat in her eyes whenever one of us did made that perfectly clear.

I didn't want that heat directed at me. It stirred up too much desire of my own.

"One deer, ready for dinner," I announced, stepping out into the grove. The other guys had already gotten a large fire crackling. Aaron was just finishing setting up a makeshift spit.

Nate grinned and moved to take the deer from me. Ren, sitting on a stone a few feet from the fire pit, wrinkled her nose. I didn't like the discomfort I saw in her eyes now either. Maybe I *should* have come out naked.

"So you just went out there and hunted it down?" she said.

I wasn't going to let myself feel ashamed about something this basic. "What, like an animal? In case you've forgotten, I am one. I did a lot worse to those vampires a couple days ago."

"Yeah, but they attacked us first." Her gaze followed the deer as Nate set it on a log to skin it. As the knife cut into the hide, she winced and looked away.

"We need to eat. We're all predators here, Sparks. This is the way of the wild." I motioned toward the deer. "I picked off one that was already lame. It wasn't fit to survive anyway. So just enjoy your meal. You can thank me after."

Ren

I drew my legs closer to my stone perch and balanced my

phone on my knees. *It's like he constantly has to be taking me down a peg,* I texted to Kylie. *He treats me like I'm an idiot.*

Boys pulling pigtails, she wrote back with a winking emoji. *He's got it for you bad.*

I glanced across the grove to where West was helping Nate arrange the deer carcass on the spit Aaron had fashioned. The firelight caught on the red and silver in his hair and the angular planes of his handsome face.

Way too handsome. Even when I was irritated with him, I couldn't squash the longing to see a real smile cross that face, directed at me.

He's twenty-seven, I replied. *I think he's past the preschool stage of flirting.*

You'd be surprised. Some guys never grow out of it. I say you march right up to him and plant one on him. And then write back to tell me all about the amazing sex you two get up to.

I shook my head at the screen. *Ha ha. Not likely.*

Oh, hey, dinner's here. Catch you again soon!

I tucked the phone into my pocket and watched the guys set the roasting stick holding *our* dinner over the fire. The flames sizzled as a few drops of blood dripped off the skinned flesh. The mass of pink and red muscle made me think of the claw marks that still hadn't quite faded from my skin. The blood in Kylie's hair last night. I rubbed my arms.

What had West said about that deer? That it'd been weak. Not fit to survive. Did he think the same thing when he looked at me? I wasn't even coming close to keeping up with my supposed mates. Marco had said a dragon shifter would put the rest of them to shame. I'd hardly been living up to that expectation.

A stick snapped in the forest behind me. I flinched and jerked around, my heart thudding. It was only Marco himself, coming back from a patrol of our campsite. He dipped his head to me with his slanted smirk. "Nothing to worry about, princess. All clear."

The thickening darkness behind him looked anything but clear. The rogue shifters might not be close enough for him to sense, but they could be tracking us. Who knew how quickly they could move? Most of the ones that had attacked me and Kylie had outrun West's kin.

Apprehension prickled over me. I hugged myself and turned back to the fire.

Marco sauntered past me and cocked his head, eyeing the spit. "Now that's a fine sight. I'm glad the rest of you are so domestic."

West snorted. Nate let out a disgruntled huff of breath. "I'd hate to see what your kills look like when you're done playing with them," he said.

Marco chuckled. "I'm a jaguar, not a house cat. And I'd bet I could have taken down a deer twice that size."

"Twice as long to cook, and more meat than we'd have time to eat. Sounds like a brilliant plan." West motioned toward the trees. "Go ahead and take a stab at it, if you've got that much to prove."

"Ah, why bother when you've already done the work for me?" The jaguar shifter lowered himself onto a log and stretched his legs out as if perfectly relaxed.

A thump from the other side of the van made me startle again. "That's Aaron coming back," Nate said, noticing. Right. The eagle shifter had been taking a turn over the landscape from above before it got too dark to spot our enemies.

He emerged from behind the van a moment later, buttoning up his shirt as he came. I couldn't help feeling a little sorry to see those sculpted muscles disappearing behind the fabric.

"See anything interesting, bird boy?" Marco asked him. He poked at the fire idly with a stick.

"Nothing worthy of immediate concern," Aaron said. "But we shouldn't lower our guards."

"No chance of that with the bunch of you."

Nate grimaced at him. "Why don't you make yourself useful and turn the damn spit, Marco?"

"Hmm, I think this side needs a little longer."

"Give me that." West grabbed the stick from him. "You're going to put out the fire at that rate." He prodded two of the logs Marco had jostled closer together. A flicker of a memory passed through my head—a brief squabble with my sisters, tug-of-war over a toy. A lump rose in my throat.

The question that had occurred to me earlier prodded me again. This seemed as good a time to ask as any.

"There are only four alphas at any time, right?" I said.

Marco gave me an amused look. "Aren't we enough for you, princess?"

I rolled my eyes at him. "I didn't mean it like that. I just meant... A dragon shifter is supposed to take the alphas as mates. So what if there's more than one dragon shifter? My sisters weren't *supposed* to die."

Aaron dipped his head. "No," he said. "And it's common for each dragon shifter to give birth to more than one daughter, in case of a tragedy. Generally speaking, your parents would have chosen which of you seemed best suited for the responsibility, and the others would have supported her. They could take mates as well, but their line wouldn't pass on."

"Oh. I guess that makes sense." So if the rogues hadn't carried out their bloody assault, it might have been one of my sisters bonded to these four now. The thought sent an uncomfortable prickling over my skin. I turned my gaze back to the fire.

The flames danced higher, nearly grazing the deer's flesh. It was starting to brown. The sizzles that reached my ears now were drips of fat, not blood. The smell of roasted venison was trickling through the air.

My mouth started to water. Maybe I didn't like the idea of killing a deer, but I wasn't too squeamish to eat it now that it was already dead. I guessed that kind of did make me a hypocrite.

The flickering light and the wavering warmth started to lull my nerves. I let my gaze sink into the fire. The flames darted up and back down, orange tinged with a darker red around the edges. Yellow-white at their core. Beautiful, the way they flared to life. Almost like—

The fragment of memory rushed up so fast it rocked me on my seat. For an instant, I was a little girl again, clutching my mother's scaled leg as the ground fell away beneath us. The swoop of her wings warbled through the air. Sharp cracks rang out below us. What was that sound? I'd never heard it before, but it terrified me.

Mama opened her dragon mouth and spewed a stream of flame at our attackers. My arm was throbbing. Blood seeped from a gouge just above my elbow. Tears streaked down my cheeks. Another burst of flame filled my vision, and—

I caught myself before I tipped right over, planting my feet hard on the ground. The heat of the campfire washed over me, sharper than before. My hand rose to my arm, to the phantom pain of that long ago wound. I rubbed the skin there even though I didn't have a scar to show it had been real.

"Ren?" Nate said from across the grove. "Are you okay?"

"I'm fine." I pushed myself to my feet. I couldn't be that little girl anymore, clinging helplessly while someone else did all the fighting. It didn't matter which of my sisters Mom and my dads would have chosen to lead. I was the only one left, and I had the ferocity in me... somewhere.

My gaze traveled up one of the tall birch trees near the edge of the grove. Its white bark shone against the darkness. Without letting myself second-guess the impulse, I strode over to it and grasped the lowest branches.

"What are you up to, princess?" Marco asked.

"Just need to stretch my legs a bit," I said. "Don't mind me."

I clambered upward from branch to branch, steadying myself when I needed to against the trunk. The papery bark rustled under my groping hands. The smells of the roasting meat and the fire fell away, leaving only the tangy scent of sap.

I stopped when the trunk had narrowed a little too much for comfort and peered down. West was turning the meat. The other guys were peering up at me, watching my progress. The firelight danced off their faces.

I was about as high up as I'd been in the pine a few days ago. A jump I knew I could make. But I didn't want to land. I wanted those wings to unfurl from my back and carry me back toward the sky.

The urge to fly had been with me my whole life. Maybe I could draw it all the way out if my body believed shifting was the only way to protect me from the fall?

I dragged in a breath. Then I launched myself out into the air.

Normally I'd have moved right into my landing pose: feet braced, knees bent, body properly aligned. But I had to believe I'd hurt myself if I hit the ground. I let my limbs scatter, a gasp slipping from my mouth as my hair whipped up behind me. I could break a leg or worse like this. If I didn't shift and glide out of the fall.

A fluttering sensation raced through my chest, but my body stayed totally human. My body careened on down. The ground looked far too close. Shit. Biting back a curse, I yanked my feet under me at the last second.

I hit the ground slightly off balance, but managed to roll out of the fall with at least a bit of grace. My left foot had taken too much of my weight. It throbbed when I straightened up. I gritted my teeth and managed to march back to my stone seat without limping.

"If you're looking for thrills, there are plenty of other activities I could suggest," Marco said, arching his eyebrows.

In what wasn't my greatest show of maturity, I stuck my tongue out at him. He laughed. He didn't seem phased by my jump, but when my gaze traveled around the fire, I realized Aaron and West were both watching me. Aaron looked thoughtful. West's eyes had narrowed. My skin itched with the suspicion that neither of them totally bought my story about "stretching my legs."

Thankfully, Nate stepped in then to distract both them and me from my continuing failure to be an actual shifter. He carved a hunk of venison off the roasting deer and offered it to me on a paper plate. "You should eat something," he said. "We're all going to need our strength."

Yeah. I dug in, closing my eyes as the smoky juices filled my mouth. Delicious. When had I ever had meat this fresh in my life?

But it couldn't quite erase the twisting in my stomach. One more attempt to shift gone down in flames —or rather, gone down *without* flames. How many more tries was I going to get?

CHAPTER 19

Ren

I'D SLEPT in a lot worse places than the seat of a fairly luxurious SUV. In corners of vacant buildings surrounded by druggies. Under ratty blankets that smelled like cat piss tucked away in an alley. On the hard concrete floor of the church basement Fisher operated out of, with a hard lump of guilt filling my stomach over the previous day's thefts and the ones I'd have to commit tomorrow.

But tonight I couldn't settle. I pulled the wool blanket West had shoved at me higher over my shoulders and squirmed against the seat back. My body refused to relax into the soft leather.

In the backseat, behind me, the low, steady murmur of Marco's breaths told me he'd had no trouble passing out. Nate was sprawled in the driver's seat, which he'd tipped back to just above my feet, his rugged face soft with sleep. West and Aaron were somewhere out in the woods on first watch.

I was surrounded by my alphas. Perfectly safe. But maybe the idea of their protection nagged at me more than it comforted me.

I closed my eyes and tried to let my mind drift away. Crickets chirped outside the window. A breeze hissed through the trees branches. The taste of roast venison lingered in my mouth. It was starting to go sour. No toothbrushes out here in the wild. I groped for the bottle of water I'd left on the car floor.

Just after I'd set it back down, a faint humming emanated from Nate's seat. He stirred and reached to his pocket to switch off the alert he must have set on his phone. As he sat up, my restlessness gripped me even harder. I couldn't stand to spend one more second shut away in the SUV, not right now.

He glanced over at me when I sat up. "I'm just going to switch off with Aaron," he said quietly. "He'll be back here in a few minutes."

"I can't sleep," I said. "I think a little walk might burn off some energy."

The corners of his eyes crinkled with concern, but he didn't try to stop me. He slipped out the driver's side door, and I eased open the back one.

The sky was clear, the stars gleaming bright against the black. I couldn't remember the last time I'd seen the constellations that clearly. In New York City, the haze of city lights always blotted out all but the most insistent stars.

I followed Nate into the woods in silence, wondering

whether he and Aaron had arranged a meeting spot or if he was just locating the eagle shifter by scent. The summer night breeze tickled past me, still pleasantly warm. We'd walked for several minutes, weaving between the trees, before a streak of moonlight caught on Aaron's golden-blond hair up ahead. He turned to greet Nate. His gaze halted on me.

"No activity so far," he said to Nate, and then to me, "I thought you'd gone to sleep."

There was no judgment in his tone, or even anything like Nate's almost suffocating concern. Just curiosity. My shoulders edged down from the argument I'd been braced for. "I tried," I said with a weak smile. "It didn't stick. I was hoping the walk would help."

"I can keep you company for that." He nodded to Nate and offered his hand to me. I took it, loving the feel of his strong fingers closing around mine.

"So has the walking helped?" he asked as we ambled back toward our campsite.

I bit my lip. I felt a little more settled with him there beside me, but that restless twitch was still nibbling at my nerves. "I don't know. Not as much as I hoped."

He ran his thumb over the back of my hand. "Do you want to talk about what's on your mind?"

"How do you know something is on my mind?"

"You can't sleep, and so you're wandering in the woods in the middle of the night. I figured it was a pretty safe guess."

I made a face at him, and he gave me an even smile. Well, it wasn't as if he was wrong. "I'm not sure talking will help either."

"It's worth a try, right?" He paused, turning me toward him. "What's bothering you?"

I looked at the ground. "I just... You've all been great. Well, West—let's not go there. The rest of you have been. And all the people in that village. Everyone is so eager to welcome me as a shifter. As the most important shifter there is. But I still can't even shift."

"It's only been a few days," Aaron said. "You're getting there."

"Maybe. It's not just that. I don't know how I can be even half of the things I'm supposed to be. What if... What if I'm ruined, because of all those years when I didn't know who I was, growing up the wrong way, without any idea about any of this? What if I *can't* ever be a full shifter?"

"Oh, Serenity." He opened his arms, and I stepped closer to him automatically. That pull, that need to be near each of the guys was getting harder to deny. He cupped my face, and I tilted my head to meet his kiss. The heat of his lips coursed through me. It didn't take away my doubts, but it was an awfully nice distraction.

After the kiss, he eased me back slightly, keeping his hands on either side of my face. His head bowed until the fringe of his hair brushed my forehead. "I'll tell you something," he said. "Something I've never really talked about with anyone. I spent most of my life wondering if I wasn't exactly what a shifter was meant to be too."

"What?" I pulled back far enough to stare into his eyes. "How could *you* think that? You're not just a shifter —you're the one chosen to be your whole kin-group's alpha."

"By a man who might have changed his mind if he'd been alive long enough to see me through to adulthood, for all I knew," Aaron said. "There are always cracks where doubt can creep in, no matter how secure your position seems. And mine never felt all that secure. The avian shifters... We're not always considered equal to the other groups. Most of the canine and feline kin see us as something lesser."

"That's ridiculous," I said. "If anything, they should be jealous. You can *fly*."

He chuckled. "Of course you'd appreciate that. But it is what it is. And even among my own people—I've told you how important it is to me to lead with my mind more than my animal side. That's not a common attitude among shifters of any kin-group. Some of my kin have been wary of my interest in learning and history. There've been more than a few who thought it meant I was making up for a lack of the 'real' strength an alpha needs to lead."

I gave him a look up and down, knowing my appreciation of his sculpted body must show in my expression. "So, those people must have been blind, I'm guessing."

Aaron's smile grew into a grin. "It's easy for people to distrust what they don't understand. But I've proven myself by now, more than once. When push came to shove, and I had the opportunity to let go—to let the alpha role pass to someone else—I knew I couldn't. That I wanted this. That I was meant for it. And here I still am."

I hesitated, remembering what he'd told me before

about how another shifter could become the alpha. "You had to fight. People challenged you?"

"Yeah." The good humor in his expression faded for a moment. He glanced away, toward the trees, recalling events I could tell he didn't enjoy thinking about. "The worst was one of my advisors. He got used to having the extra authority. When I turned twenty-one and was meant to take over my full role as alpha, he attacked me. I hated having to fight him. He'd been like an uncle to me. But I was smarter and faster, and that can beat brutality if you know how to use it."

"And here you still are," I said, repeating his words back to him.

"Here I am." He drew his gaze back to me. Right then it was so intense I almost forgot how to breathe. My heart thumped faster.

He wasn't just strong and overwhelmingly sexy. He was *good*. Thoughtful and brave and compassionate. The kind of man I'd never been sure I'd be able to have in my life. The kind of man I could fall in love with.

Not just could. I was already falling. Right into those clear blue eyes.

"Well, as far as I'm concerned, anyone who thinks you're anything less than those other guys is an idiot," I said, for something to say. "As well as being blind."

"Probably," Aaron said agreeably. "I don't worry about it anymore. And I find it equally hard to believe that anyone could be around you and think you're anything less than a true shifter. It's in your blood. That's all that matters. The rest will fall into place."

My fingers had curled into the front of his shirt without my even noticing. I tugged, and he came to me.

He kissed me hard this time, nudging me a step backward so I could lean against the trunk of a tree. So I didn't even have to think about staying upright, only about the heat of his body against me and the slide of his mouth against mine. His hand traveled down my side to my thigh and back up to my shoulder, as if he wasn't sure what part of me he wanted to touch most.

Everywhere. I wanted him everywhere.

His hips brushed mine, and an ache started to form between my legs. Where Nate had gotten me off so skillfully less than a day ago. I whimpered as Aaron stroked my breast through another kiss, but one last thread of uncertainty held me back.

I grasped the side of Aaron's face. He eased back to meet my gaze. His was full of desire, so hot every nerve inside me caught fire.

My voice came out ragged. "You don't mind, do you, that it's not just you? That I'm supposed to be with the other guys too?" That I had been, in ways he'd witnessed or at least sensed.

Aaron bumped his nose against mine in an affectionate nuzzle. "Not at all," he murmured. "You deserve nothing less. It takes more than one man to satisfy a dragon." His fingers teased up under my shirt. I arched my back off the tree trunk to give him room to unclasp my bra. He circled my nipple with his thumb before flicking right over it with a speed that made me gasp.

"You deserve every bit of pleasure they can give you,"

he went on, moving to caress my other breast. He kissed the corner of my jaw, the sensitive skin of my throat. His words spilled out with his heated breath. "Anything that fulfills you, whoever it's with, fulfills me too. The flush in your cheeks after you've been kissed. The sound you make when you come."

So he had heard Nate and me in the back of the car. My face outright flared. But, God, Aaron was turning me on so much with every graze of his lips, every stroke of his fingers.

"I'm looking forward to someday seeing how much pleasure we can bring you together," he said. "But for now…"

His hands slid down my body. I whimpered, my hips canting toward his. Seeking every inch of contact I could get.

"I need to see you," he muttered. He yanked my shirt up. I raised my arms so he could pull it off in one smooth movement. My bra slid from my shoulders to fall to the ground by our feet. Aaron took me in, my smallish breasts with the nipples pebbled from his attentions, the flush creeping down between them. Then he ducked his head to suck one of those peaks into his mouth.

I moaned, pleasure racing over my skin. His steady tongue slicked over my breast with the slightest graze of his teeth, until I was trembling against him, my fingers tangled in his hair. He gave the nipple one last lick before attending to my other breast with equal enthusiasm.

It wasn't nearly enough for the hunger inside me. I grasped the hem of his shirt. "Off," I gasped. "Now."

He wrenched it over his head faster than I'd have

thought possible, with the snap of at least one button. Somehow that turned me on even more. I seemed to have no limit when it came to these guys.

He claimed my mouth again with an urgent fervor. The press of his bare chest against mine drew another moan out of me. My fingernails sketched lines up the muscles of his back. He hefted me as if I weighed nothing at all, bracing me higher against the tree with one hand supporting my ass and my legs splayed. I gripped my thighs around his. The hard length of him pressed against my core, and I whimpered.

Aaron rocked against me as he leaned in for another, even deeper kiss. I could feel the strength coiled all through him, holding me up, but also braced to withdraw the second I told him to stop. Pleasure rushed through me, but suddenly the sweep of it didn't feel unnerving at all.

I was exactly where I wanted to be. I belonged here, with this man, in every way he wanted to be with me.

Giving in to my desires wasn't letting go of control. It was taking it. Grasping hold of the destiny I'd never imagined and claiming it as *mine*.

The second I made the decision, a hum of power rose up inside me, stronger than I'd ever felt before. I linked my arms behind Aaron's neck and dipped my head between one kiss and the next.

"I want this," I said, breathless, "I want *you*."

He hesitated, searching my eyes, a wildness in his. "Do you mean—"

"Aaron," I said, as clearly as I could manage. "Be my mate?"

A strangled laugh burst out of him, as if he couldn't quite believe what I'd said. He crushed his mouth against mine, kissing me until I was dizzy. I fumbled with the button of his slacks. My hand brushed over his erection, and he groaned.

"I think we'd better take this to the ground," he said, guiding me away from the tree. He grabbed his shirt and stretched it over the dirt before he laid me down in it. "For our first time, anyway."

"Lots of time to experiment later," I said, and his eyes flashed even hotter. He kicked off his pants. I couldn't wait to touch his cock. The huge, hard length of him pulsed against my palm through his boxers.

Aaron bowed his head, exhaling with a stutter. Holding himself over me with one arm, he dipped the other hand down between my legs. A mewing sound escaped me as he stroked me there. My breath broke into panting as he slipped his fingers under the band of my sweatpants. My sex was already slick with my arousal. He trailed his hand over that wetness and muffled another groan in my hair.

"Please," I said. He didn't need me to beg more than that. He jerked off my pants and panties together and wrenched off his boxers. My hips arched up as he settled between my legs. The head of his cock rubbed over my opening. I pulled his mouth back to mine.

He kissed me and eased inside at the same time. His hardness filled me with a burning sensation, but it was oh so good. I was filled, completely, and it was everything I needed.

"You feel amazing, Serenity," he murmured between

kisses. He lifted my hips higher and thrust into me with a steadily building rhythm. I clung on to him as the swell of pleasure carried me higher. Up and up, until it shuddered through my whole body. Until I barely felt the ground beneath me.

We were flying. Soaring up and away on a haze of bliss. No leap or fall had come close to comparing to this exhilaration.

His cock nudged against the sweetest spot inside me, and the bliss shattered apart. It radiated through my entire body, tossing me even higher. I gasped, digging my fingernails into his shoulders. Sparks flared behind my fluttering eyelids. The pull between us solidified into a solid glow that bound us together. It lit me up like a flare from the inside.

Aaron's thrusts turned erratic. He pumped into me a few more times and moaned as he followed me over the edge. His body settled over mine, resting against me but not pinning me down. Every inch of his naked skin aligned with mine.

I traced my fingers back up his neck and into his sweat-damp hair to draw him down for one last kiss. My muscles trembled with release—and happiness.

I had him. My eagle shifter. My alpha.

My mate.

Ren

I woke up cuddled against Aaron on the middle seat of the SUV. Daylight was streaming through the windows. My head still felt fuzzy from not quite enough sleep, and various parts of my body ached, but in an enjoyable way. I had no desire at all to get up.

I buried my head into the crook of Aaron's neck. The wonderful salty fresh smell of his skin filled my nose. We'd gotten dressed before we'd finally made it the rest of the way back to the car, but I hadn't been quite ready to let go of him yet. It was a tight fit, our legs intertwined and him half on top of me, and yet I felt totally at home tangled there with him.

My mate. The knowledge thrummed through my veins. Only the first, if I fulfilled my role completely, but right now one was plenty.

Knuckles rapped against the window over my head. I

blinked and peered up at it. Aaron brushed a kiss to my temple before raising his head.

Marco looked in at us, his eyebrows arched. He opened the door a few inches to talk. "Wolf boy found us some eggs. You'd better get up if you want to grab them before our resident bear eats them all."

"I'm leaving plenty for the rest of you," Nate said from somewhere behind him. Marco dipped his head and shut the door again.

Did his expression look a little tighter than usual? Something about his stance had felt off. *He* wasn't upset seeing me with Aaron, was he? He knew how this was supposed to work just as well as the others did.

Probably it was my insecurities messing with my head. Out of the four guys, Marco seemed the *least* likely to get possessive. The way he carried himself, the way he talked, I was pretty sure he hadn't let a little discomfort stop him from enjoying all the pleasures of the body with other women while he'd waited those sixteen years for me.

Aaron straightened up, tugging me with him. He slid his fingers into my hair and kissed me again, on the lips this time. His mouth lingered against mine just long enough for me to start wishing we could launch into a sequel to last night's activities right now. Then he pulled back with a sheepish smile. His blond hair was delightfully rumpled. I couldn't resist ruffling it a little more for good measure.

He laughed. "I guess we really should get some breakfast. We don't know what's waiting for us in Sunridge."

Right. My giddiness faded as nervous anticipation coiled around my gut. I clambered out of the van. Nate looked up from where he was scraping at fried eggs on a metal sheet over the fire, the corners of his lips curling up when he caught my eye. Oh, he knew what I'd gotten up to with Aaron last night, all right. And from the slant of West's eyebrows as he very definitely *didn't* meet my eyes, it was obvious the wolf shifter did too.

Well, we hadn't exactly tried to hide our new intimacy. What else did I expect? It was only going to get weirder as I accepted each of the others as mates too... whenever I felt ready to do that.

I had plenty of other bigger concerns to tackle first. "How far off are we from Sunridge?" I asked the camp at large.

Aaron got out his phone to check the map, but West spoke up first. "About two hours, depending on the roads. Are you in a hurry, Sparks?"

I gave him a pointed look. "I've been wanting to know what happened to my mother for seven years, *Wolfie*. So yeah, I might be a little impatient."

Marco snickered at the nickname, and Nate covered a guffaw. West glowered at me. "I guess you'd better get eating then."

Nate handed me a plate, and I gulped down the flame-cooked eggs with one of the rolls the villagers had sent us off with. We piled into the SUV, West and Aaron taking their original places up front. "Come join me, Princess of Flames," Marco said, patting the middle seat beside him, so I did. As Nate climbed into the back and West started the ignition, the jaguar shifter squeezed my knee briefly—just long enough to send a spark of heat up my leg.

Marco grinned at me, looking more relaxed now. I smiled back, but the view beyond the windshield pulled my gaze away. Down the road, where the forest thinned, tall mountains rose. A faint dusting of snow gleamed on the highest of the dark gray peaks. Sunridge lay just beyond that first range.

"Have you remembered anything that might explain why your mom sent us on this little road trip?" Macro asked.

I shook my head. "I don't think she ever mentioned Wyoming. Are there any important shifter communities nearby?"

"Not that I'm aware of. But I'm sure the dragon shifters kept a few secrets to themselves."

He took my hand as we drove on, idly trailing his fingers back and forth over my palm, but he didn't push for any more contact than that. As much as I enjoyed the warmth of his touch, I was too distracted to *want* more.

Two hours, and I might finally get some answers. I might even see Mom again. The jitters of anticipation returned, fluttering around my stomach.

West eased on the gas as the road narrowed. It veered up, winding along a pass between two of the mountains. Stray rocks rattled against the SUV's undercarriage. The sunlight dimmed, hidden behind the southern peak.

"There's someone on the road," Aaron said. West slowed the car even more. He hit the button to lower his window and inhaled to scent the air. I leaned forward, peering between the front seats. A figure was standing in our lane a few hundred feet ahead of us—a young guy who didn't look much past his teens.

"He's one of us," West said. "Feline from the smell of him." He glanced back at Marco. "Do you know him?"

"Right," Marco drawled. "Because all us feline-kin must know each other." He narrowed his eyes. "No, he doesn't look familiar, but that doesn't mean much."

"Can you tell if he's one of the rogues?" I asked. "How do you know who's kin and who isn't?"

"Kin take a mark of loyalty, like our alpha mark, on their palms," Aaron said. "If someone once kin goes rogue, the mark fades. We'll need to get closer to know."

"I don't like this," Nate said from behind me. "It's too much of a coincidence."

"I don't like it either," West said. "But some of my kin back in the village knew where we were headed. They might have passed on word if there was bad news from another group. I can't just run the guy over without knowing."

"Well, you could," Marco said. "If he's anyone's kin, he's mine. You have my full permission to plow right into him. If he's got half a survival instinct, he'll jump out of the way in time."

"Right," West said with an obvious edge of sarcasm. "That'll really improve kin-group relations."

Marco dragged in a breath. "Whatever you want, wolf boy. He's just a bobcat. I'm sure between the four of us we can take him if we need to."

But could we take whatever allies the stranger might have lurking nearby? My body tensed as we came up on the guy, the SUV rolling to a stop. I scanned the mountainside along the road. Nothing moved, but there were way too many crags and boulders that could be concealing an enemy.

The guy started ambling toward the car. West glanced back at Marco. "As you pointed out, *jaguar boy*, he'd be your kin. You go talk to him. If something goes wrong, I'm sure you can jump right back in the car as we speed out of here."

His voice was dry, but a thread of tension ran through it. He'd left one hand on the steering wheel, gripping it tightly. Aaron eyed the guy through the windshield. In the back seat, Nate undid his seatbelt. Preparing in case he needed to shift, I guessed. We were all on high alert.

Marco muttered something about "ungrateful canines," but he got up and slid open the door. "Stay right there, princess," he told me. He hopped out and sauntered up the road to meet the stranger. "Kin mark?" he asked.

The guy started to raise his hand—and two sharp *cracks* split the air. The same sharp, echoing sound I'd heard in my memory of my mother's desperate flight with me from our old home.

The SUV hitched, with a sputtering sound from one of the tires. Marco's shoulder jerked. He stumbled sideways, clutching his chest just below his collarbone. Blood bloomed beneath his fingers.

My heart stopped. Gunshots. That's what that sound was.

The rogues didn't care about shifter law, obviously. They'd brought guns to this fight—and to that one long ago.

"Marco!" West hollered. He pressed on the gas pedal, but the deflated tire thumped weakly against the pavement. "Shit. I'll get him. Stay low."

He threw himself out of the driver's seat before anyone could protest. Another bullet struck the window across from me. The glass cracked. I flinched down, ducking beside the seat. Nate growled. Aaron wrenched off his shirt.

"You're going to shift?" I said, panic jolting through me. "They'll shoot you out there." Two more *cracks* rang out, with a *thunk* against the side of the SUV—and a snarl on the road outside. Where was West? Had he gotten to Marco? How many rogues were in on this ambush?

"It's a lot harder to hit a moving target," Aaron said. He shot me a quick look, his bright eyes intent. "Stay down. We'll take care of this."

He leapt out, slamming the door behind him. A flash of golden feathers rocketed past the window an instant later.

A hiss and a yelp carried from down the road. My alphas or the rogues? I didn't dare raise my head high enough to peek out the window.

"And it takes more than a few bullets to stop a bear," Nate growled. He shoved open the back hatch, shifting as he went. His immense furry body charged past my window into the fray.

Another shot crackled. I winced, my fingernails digging into the leather seat. My heart thudded so fast the beats blended together.

A voice, thick and guttural, called out from

somewhere above. "Give up the dragon shifter, kin-bound, and you'll live to keep bossing your people around."

The words struck a chord of recognition deep down in the animal core of me. I'd never heard that voice speak before, but it jolted me back to the first rogue attack, the snarls and growls of the black wolf that had tried to gouge open my neck. The skin there stung in memory.

I swallowed hard. He must be the one leading this group. But my alphas obviously weren't interested in bargaining my life away. The snaps and cries from down the road were getting louder.

A high keening filled the air—Aaron's battle cry—and cut off abruptly. My throat constricted.

The rogues had killed four alphas once before. My fathers. They'd murdered my sisters too. Slaughtered almost all of the people who'd mattered most to me. And now they were trying to take away my mates too, to get at me.

No. Rage bubbled up inside me. My fingers curled tighter, forming fists. I dragged in a breath, slow and steady the way Aaron had taught me, and the anger streamed through me in a white hot glow. As powerful as the connection that had solidified between him and me when I'd claimed him as mine last night. When I'd grasped the role I was meant for with both hands.

The energy rippled through all my limbs. I was not going to let this happen again. Not here. Not now. I would not *stay*. My alphas deserved a mate who could protect them as much as they protected me.

And damn it, they had one.

I dashed forward to grasp the door handle. Yanking the side door open, I flung myself out of the car. Out and *up*.

The shift rippled through my muscles, stretching, burning. My body expanded, sleek and sinewy. Talons ripped from my arched fingers. Wings burst from my back. They flapped with an instinctive heft, and I careened through the air. My eyes sharpened. The wind warbled over the smooth scales covering my skin. Fire smoldered all through my extended neck.

I'd done it. I was a dragon. And it felt *amazing*.

I beat my wings, soaring higher. Testing every inch of my newfound body. But I didn't have time to savor the sensations. My shadow streaked over the ground, twice as large as the SUV, and my gaze caught on a woman crouched by a boulder thirty feet up the mountainside. A pistol was braced in her hands. She raised it toward me.

A fiery confidence blazed through me. Oh, no. She could forget that. She was going to regret ever messing with me and mine.

I dove toward her. She pulled the trigger. A splinter of pain lanced through one of my wings, but I didn't care. I opened my jaws and let loose the fire searing through me.

The woman screamed as the flames engulfed her. I swooped over her hiding spot and whipped around, seeking out her companions. There'd been two guns firing. Where was the other coward hiding behind a pistol?

There. A gray-haired man hunkered down in a

crevice on the other side of the road, not a pistol but a rifle poised against the dark rock. I swung toward him.

He proved himself an even bigger coward. Dropping the gun, he shifted into a black-and-gray-speckled weasel and darted away up the mountain.

I sped after the weasel shifter, but he dove into a deeper crevice. I blasted it with fire and then spun around. My gaze narrowed on a man with shaggy black hair who was leaping to snatch up the rifle.

"Keep at them, keep at them!" he hollered down the slope in the same guttural voice I'd heard demanding that my alphas hand me over. His scent laced the air with a wolfish tang. It was him. The rogue who'd left me marked all over with the slashes of his claws. Who'd led his followers to savage Kylie too.

Anger surged up inside me. I was never letting him get a chance like that again.

The wolf shifter swung toward me, yanking the rifle upward, as if he thought he might catch me by surprise. A hot, heavy blast of dragon-fire was already searing up my throat. I opened my jaws and let it flow.

My fury blasted over the rogue's leader, leaving nothing but a charred heap and the molten lump of the rifle where he'd been. A twist of brutal satisfaction filled my chest.

I wheeled toward the road. A few of the other rogues were already fleeing, racing up the mountainside the way they'd come. The young man who'd stopped our SUV sprawled on the pavement, his chest torn and his throat gashed open. My wolf and my eagle had pinned a black bear to the ground between them. My grizzly was cuffing a mountain lion across the head. It bolted away as my shadow swept over them. I couldn't see Marco.

I turned again, meaning to give chase, and a prickling sensation raced through my muscles. They were clenching, condensing, the effort of the shift catching up with me. I strained to hold my shape, but exhaustion gripped me.

It was my first time. I had no stored endurance.

Gritting my teeth, I plummeted to the ground.

CHAPTER 21

Aaron

Serenity!

The shout echoed in my head as I saw her brilliant body fall from the sky. My eagle's throat couldn't form the name. My talons loosened where I gripped the bear's shoulder, the urge to fly to her rushing through me.

The black bear had gone limp in my and West's grasp, but now it lashed out its paw in one last desperate smack. Its claws raked across one of my wings. A lance of pain joined the other aches already radiating through my body.

I bobbed to the side and slashed at the bear, torn between two duties. Nate lumbered over, baring his teeth threateningly at the rogue that could have been his kin. He swung his head toward me as if to say, *Go on*.

My wounded wing faltered as I pushed myself backward. I landed awkwardly on my clawed feet and shifted back into human form. Bleeding claw marks scored my right arm, and a burning gash ran across my ribs. Clenching my jaw against the discomfort, I pushed myself toward my mate.

Serenity had hit the pavement on her hands and knees, somewhere between human and dragon form. The dragon side of her had saved her from the worst of the impact. She was slumped a few feet from the SUV when my eyes found her, and my pulse lurched.

Before I'd even dashed two steps, she raised her head. A bullet wound was leaking blood down her forearm and a scrape marked her chin from the impact, but her amber eyes glinted with a deeper fire than I'd ever seen before. It took my breath away.

I dropped to my knees beside her and pulled her to me. She sagged into my embrace, her cheek against my collarbone. Her chest was still heaving with ragged breaths.

"You were fantastic," I said, stroking my hand over her dark hair. "The most spectacular thing I've ever seen." My heart swelled with the memory of her bright red scales flashing against the sky.

My mate. My dragon shifter. And she'd accepted me as her own last night. The awe of it filled my throat.

Serenity's hand brushed over my wounded arm and stilled. She pushed herself upright. Her eyes widened. "You're hurt. We have to get you bandaged up. Is everyone else okay?"

"We all survived," I said. "And I'll heal." But she was right. I'd lost more than enough blood already. I heaved myself to my feet, reluctant to leave her. Moving to the car, I grabbed my pants and tossed my shirt to her, since her own had ripped apart with her transformation. The shreds of it lay on the road by the open door.

There was a roll of sterile gauze in the glove compartment for exactly this eventuality. I wrapped up my arm and knelt beside Serenity to tend to her own wound. She winced as I covered it.

"Fucking bullets. That's how they came after my family before. I heard the shots in one of my memories, just didn't realize what they were until now."

The set of my mouth hardened. "It's a stark line for them to cross. Any shifter who's broken that law, used a weapon against their own kind, can never join a kin-group in future."

"I get the impression that lot is more interested in tearing apart our groups than joining them," Marco said, propping himself against the hood of the car. He'd balled his own shirt against the bullet hole on his upper chest. The wound hadn't stopped him from shifting into jaguar form and taking care of the bobcat shifter who'd tricked us and then attacked him. Nate had shoved him toward the shelter of the SUV after that.

"Rogues don't usually like to completely throw away their other options," I muttered. Serenity moved to stand, and I straightened up with her.

West and Nate had both shifted back. So had the black bear shifter, who was now a woman sprawled limply on the road. The blankness of her half-open eyes dampened my relief. "She's dead." Damn.

"She took one of the bullets meant for us," West said, nodding to a bloody mark on her chest. "Managed to fight like she wasn't dying for long enough despite it." Bloody scores marked his chest, just below the glowing splatter of a scar I knew had been left by fae magic. He hurried to the SUV to grab his clothes, shooting me a pained look as he passed. "I was hoping we'd get some answers too."

Our dragon shifter was staring at the woman. She bit her lip. She'd taken lives with her dragon-fire a few minutes ago, but seeing a dead body up close wasn't something Serenity was used to.

"I got their leader," she said, jerking her gaze away. "The wolf shifter who attacked me in the village. He's a pile of ashes up there now." She jabbed her hand toward the mountain slope. "I tried to catch the ones that were running too…"

Nate's eyes darkened. "You did everything you could, Ren. I've never seen any other shifter hold their form that long the first time they made a full transition."

"Oh." She blinked. Then a small smile crossed her lips.

Nate followed West to the car. We had to get moving before any humans showed up. The road wasn't frequently traveled and we'd left the last town several miles behind, but that didn't mean there hadn't been anyone around to hear the gunshots.

Serenity pulled my shirt closer around her shoulders. "They still wanted me dead," she said.

"Apparently sixteen years of chaos wasn't enough for them," West muttered.

Marco's lips curled. "You put them right in their place, though, princess. Blasted them all to cinders."

We couldn't know what other rogues might be out

there who were just as set on destruction, but I didn't want to say that. Not as I watched Serenity draw her back a little straighter. She glanced around at us as the others returned, looking every bit a princess in that moment. Every bit a queen. This was a victory, and it belonged to her. I felt, in the hum of energy passing between us, my alpha equals responding to her power.

We were all in this, all the way. None of us were backing down, not even West. It felt good. It felt *right*.

"Then let's get on with whatever the rogues were trying to stop us from doing here," Serenity said. "There's just one thing I need to do first."

She turned to me and reached to cup my jaw, pulling me into a kiss I was more than happy to return. I kissed her back with all the passion and reverence I had in me, until a tremble passed through her body. Everything—the danger, the wounds just starting to heal across my body— was worth it for this.

Ren

I eased back from Aaron, breathless, but I wasn't done yet. I reached for Marco next. My jaguar shifter came easily, sliding his arm around my waist as he tipped his face to mine. He kissed me long and deep, with a teasing caress of his tongue. Of course Marco would slip that in.

Nate was there waiting for me when I stepped back from Marco. I joined my hands behind the bear shifter's neck, and he pulled me up to meet him with his broad arms. His kiss was firm but sweet, with a lingering brush of his lips over mine before he let me go.

Last I turned to my wolf shifter. West's stance had tensed. He eyed me warily, but heat smoldered inside his gaze. He wanted me, despite himself. We all felt the same pull.

I held out my hand to him. "It's just a kiss, not a contract. I need to know you're with me at least that much."

He wet his lips. The gesture sent a flicker of desire through me. "All right, Sparks," he said. "You can have your kiss."

After that, I expected him to give me nothing but the briefest of pecks. He stepped closer, bringing the smells of the forest with him, rich earth and sharp pine. My heart beat a little faster. He bowed his head, and I bobbed up on my toes to tentatively press my mouth to his.

A hungry sound reverberated in his chest. His hand found my waist, hot as a brand as he yanked me to him. He kissed me so fiercely that my head spun. For an instant, there was nothing but the heat of him and the demanding pressure of his lips.

West released me just as abruptly. He backed up, folding his arms over his chest in a familiar standoffish pose. "Let's go then," he said gruffly, holding my gaze for a moment before jerking his away.

The sharp taste of him lingered on my lips. I let out my breath, feeling as if I'd finally fully settled into my body. The body of a dragon shifter, surrounded by the four alphas who'd be my mates. "Yes," I said. "Let's."

After a brief delay while Nate and West swapped out the shot tire with the spare from the back, we set off down the road again. The mountains pulled back around a wide valley with a glittering river down its center. Sunridge lay on the south bank, a small town of a few thousand inhabitants. I peered out the window as we cruised down the main street, waiting for something to hit me.

Aaron glanced at me expectantly. I shook my head. "Nothing."

"They've got a town historical museum," Nate said, pointing. "That seems like a good place to start."

West parked outside the repurposed house. The woman at the front desk looked at us curiously as we walked in. Her badge marked her as a volunteer for the Sunridge Historical Society. How much history could a town this size have?

We wandered between the displays: weathered newspaper articles, old black and white photos, pieces of clothing belonging to some particularly exceptional mayor who as far as I could tell had simply built a new bridge over the river. Not exactly gripping stuff. I was about to call it quits when my gaze caught on a painting that filled one corner of the back wall.

My pulse stuttered. I walked up to it, a strange feeling of recognition prickling through me. I'd never seen the image before, but somehow I felt as if I knew it.

It was a simple design showing the sprawl of the snowcapped mountains. But in the center, between two of the ridges, a spark shot up like a flame toward the sky. I reached for it, catching myself just short of touching the canvas.

"Do you like that?" the historical volunteer asked, coming up behind me. She gave me a soft smile. "It's an interpretation of a larger piece in the town square, if you want to see the original."

"Yes," I said, so enthusiastically her eyebrows twitched up. "Where's that?"

"It's a quick walk from here," she said. "Just take a left when you go out, walk two blocks, then another left and you'll see the square."

"Thanks!" I rushed for the door. The guys fell in behind me.

"Did you find something?" Nate asked.

"I think so. Come on."

I hurried down the street along the route the woman had given me. We stepped into a tiny cobblestone square with only a few buildings on each side and an inn at the far end. In the middle of the square stood a dark gray stone obelisk, twinkling with specks of mica. It towered at least half again as tall as me. The same image from the painting was carved into its flat surface.

It drew me to it until I was close enough to touch. This time I let myself lay my hand on the cool stone surface. It seemed to tremble beneath my palm.

A crash of memory swept the world away.

No, not memory. Because the image of my mother that rose before my eyes wasn't one I'd ever seen before. She was standing in front of that obelisk, her brown hair shining in the sun, wearing the same dress she'd had on the last time I'd seen her. My chest squeezed.

She'd left this message for me seven years ago, when she'd stood in this exact same spot.

"Serenity," she said, her bright voice wavering from right inside my ears. "I wish I had more time to say everything I should, but I don't know how far ahead of them I've managed to stay. So all I can tell you is this: I want to give you everything you need to survive the many challenges I know are ahead of you. Our people left a power in this place centuries ago. If I haven't returned to bring it to you, there's still a chance you can retrieve it yourself. For you to have made it this far, you must be so strong already."

She touched the image of the flame between the mountains. "Here is where you'll find it. Your dragon nature will help you follow the path." Then she gazed straight into my eyes. "I love you. Never forget that."

The image wisped away. I found myself braced against the stone, my eyes swimming with tears.

"Ren?" Nate said tentatively.

I inhaled shakily and swiped at my eyes. "I'm okay," I said. "I know what we need to do. I know why my mother sent us here. There's something here I need if we're going to fix all the damage the rogues have caused."

I backed up, looking at the picture and then the mountain ranges around us. There. I stopped when my gaze settled on a matching pair of peaks. The sun was high above them now, but it would gleam between them like a flame when it was first rising. I raised my hand.

"We're going up that mountain."

Eva Chase lives in Canada with her family. She loves stories both swoony and supernatural, and strong women and the men who appreciate them. Along with the Dragon Shifter's Mates series, she is the author of the Demons of Fame Romance series and the Legends Reborn trilogy. You can visit her online at www.evachase.com.

www.ingramcontent.com/pod-product-compliance
Lightning Source LLC
Chambersburg PA
CBHW021328190726
48288CB00003B/1001